Finding Zachariah

In a Community Garden

By
Nancy Hicks Marshall

eBook ISBN: 978-0-9828259-6-9
Paperback ISBN: 978-0-9828259-7-6
Ingram Spark ISBN: 978-0-9828259-8-3
Library of Congress Control Number:

Editor: Nancy Hicks Marshall
Illustrator: Marie Provine
Cover Designer: Angie Ayala
Interior Design: Marigold2k
Publisher: Nugget Press
Support Publisher: Spotlight Publishing House

www.NuggetPress.com

Early Praise for
FINDING ZACHARIAH

What a wonderful book!

Being a cat owner and a gardener, this book truly hit the spot for me. But Nancy Marshall added so much more with all the characters and their stories. Her writing style allowed me to picture the garden in my mind.

I appreciated the cat's humor and the heartfelt emotion of a family, the community, and as an animal lover. The added informational content about plants, animals and insects was a real bonus.

—Joanne Itow
Community Gardener, Member and Volunteer, Japanese Friendship Garden, Phoenix, AZ

Beautifully Done...

Who knew a feral cat named Sebastian could observe and share so many different insights about human behavior within a Community Garden? The cat takes us into a microcosm of our world with a positive perspective while facing the pain that life can present. Recidivism has become a good thing in the Community Garden. The story's conclusion will open the mind and lighten the heart, displaying love of creation — whether planting a vegetable seed or a seed of hope.

The description of soil enrichment, appropriate plantings, and irrigation in the desert are accurate for our climate zone.

FINDING ZACHARIAH is well told, entertaining, informative and thought provoking. For those with questions, look for the Glossary, questions to explore, and a plant guide at the end.

—**Steve Orcutt**, Agriculture and Horticulture, Arizona State University; University of Arizona Agriculture and Extension programs; member and Presenter, Rare Fruit Growers Association.
—**Marilee Orcutt**, Past Arizona Brain Injury Representative to the Veteran's Administration; Volunteer working with individuals with PTSD; Certified Music Teacher; Music Therapy and Visualization Services with Veterans Suffering Trauma.

Refreshing Perspective on Tough Issues

In her latest novel, *"Finding Zachariah in a Community Garden,"* Nancy Hicks Marshall tells the transformative story of a community garden emerging from a vacant lot in South Phoenix, through the eyes of a whimsical feral cat. The story's titular (human) character, Zachariah, finds solace and companionship with the feline narrator on an abandoned couch — as he confronts his PTSD from the war in Afghanistan, alcoholism, and homelessness and attempts to piece his life back together and reclaim the love of his wife and children. Through a rich narrative, Marshall offers a refreshing perspective on tough issues.

The story unfolds into a heartfelt blend of community, redemption, and reconciliation. Readers will find it hard to put this one down, perhaps pausing only to pick up a garden trowel.

—**Steven Cusumano,** Community Gardener, Veteran Naval Aviator, Goodyear, AZ

Another Winner

Planted between the lines of this lovely little story, narrated by a feral feline, are so many lessons: how to create a community, how to plan and nurture a garden, a few healthy recipes, and — most important by far — that both food scraps and human beings are capable of being upcycled — ready for a better use. Another winner from Nancy Marshall.

—**Cindy Yurth**, Retired Journalist, Colorado.

Tugged at My Heartstrings

Nancy Marshall's story, *FINDING ZACHARIAH*, was quite moving, drawing tears on several occasions. I'm a cat guy and a veteran, plus marriage difficulties have been a theme in my life, so all three tugged at my heartstrings. Plus, personally volunteering in a community garden and having developed relationships with people who put their good sweat and tears into the garden made an emotional impact on me.

The veteran portrayal and his struggles were accurate. I've witnessed the healing power a veteran friend has experienced from volunteering in a community garden and believe others can also benefit.

—**Gary Streeter**, Arizona Air National Guard veteran, Phoenix Service Platoon Leader, The Mission Continues, Phoenix, Arizona.

The Importance of Connecting with Neighbors

I have loved reading **FINDING ZACHARIAH**. It is written from a wonderfully unique perspective. Nancy Marshall has developed her characters beautifully. The story she has cultivated perfectly illustrates the importance of connecting with neighbors through community gardens. Well done!

—**Francie Randolph,** community gardener, visual artist, and Founding Director, Sustainable CAPE, Truro, MA

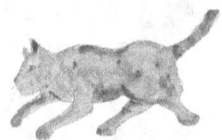

From Outcast to Deep Friendship

Sebastian, a feral cat, is an outcast — born and orphaned in a 20-acre wild, abandoned lot. Yet his curiosity and a warm heart for someone (a human) who is also an outcast leads him to a deep friendship — and leads us through a heartwarming story about life on a piece of outcast land. Through Sebastian's eyes we learn about trusting others, Mother Earth's cycle of life, and how to grow community, food, hope and healing. He also shows us how to let go of fear, be comfortable playing a larger part where we are and how life is so much better if we are open to sharing it with a friend.

—**Tom Cameron, Ph.D**. Materials Science, CT
Always photographing life, learning how things grow, friending pollinators, loving Earth

FINDING ZACHARIAH
In a Community Garden

Dedicated to
The Memory of
JOE GRAY
My Mentor by Example

and

GORDON "GORDO" DANA HICKS, 1938–1992
Captain, United States Marine Corps, 1959–1963

Contents

Chapter 1

And the Award Goes to...

All the V.I.P.S are here, jostling for a premier spot near Big Joe — and the microphone. It's the last Saturday in May. The humans call it Memorial Day weekend. It's exactly one year — to the day — since the creation of the community garden.

Ms. Mayor presses down the wrinkles in her skirt. Mr. Bank CEO straightens his tie. Captain Chris, from the Veterans' group, sports a matching 'camo' (short for camouflage) shirt and trousers. Mr. University President, wearing a 'Community Garden' T-shirt and cut-off jeans, plays casual. A priest, a rabbi, a mullah and a minister act all chummy together. Big Joe, in cargo shorts and a double-XL T-shirt — wields the mic.

But the main players — the ones who really made this a community garden — stand back. CeCe (short for Cecilia) holds court with some buyers at the veggie table while her mom, Otoña, handles the cash box at the end of the table. Zorro, CeCe's fraternal twin brother, plugs in the synthesizer with music maestro Hurricane, who provides electronic jazz-rock, country western and hip-hop at key moments during the festivities.

And Zachariah, my first and best friend, stands by the entrance to the dirt-floor pavilion, shaded by the tan tarps that serve as a roof and sunshield — grateful to be part of the community garden.

Marley stands right next to him. You'll meet Marley later.

CeCe and Zorro are a lot alike. They're twins, duh! Two weeks ago, on Smoothie Saturday, they turned thirteen — old enough to claim independent paths, *and* old enough to think about whether boys, or girls, are interesting — or not. They exhibited all that 'opposites resist & attract' behavior at the Saturday Smoothies fest. Boys on one side, girls on the other, all clamoring for the same smoothie.

They're also different. (Duh!) Zorro's a boy, CeCe's a girl. Zorro's dark — like the bark of a mesquite tree after the rain — and taller, with tight curly hair hidden under a backward ball cap. CeCe's more like the inside of a willow branch — a mellow tan — with a mahogany ponytail bouncing when she walks. Zorro likes music, CeCe likes animals. She's stubborn, he has a wild hair. That's how they differ. But they both love art. And they both love their mom — and their dad. Plus, they are the key players in this community garden. You'll meet them soon.

Zachariah shepherds a flock of almost-gonna-be or have-been juvenile delinquents who hover around him near the public library table. He commands respect among his rag-tag work crew. He's worked his way up to be a kind of job foreman, knowing the ins and outs of dirt, water, weeding and feeding. It was not always so.

There's Big Joe, of course. Without him, this garden wouldn't exist. And most of the people who come here and tend their individual garden plots keep coming back because of Big Joe. They are the recidivists. He'll explain later.

Joe schmoozes with the dignitaries.

I'm Sebastian, the feral cat. I know everyone. I know who's done the most (besides me) to convert this abandoned lot into a community garden. It is definitely not the mayor, the bank CEO or the University President, or even Captain Chris.

The time has come to announce the award. I watch Big Joe, who smiles at all the families. He takes an extra moment to lock eyes with CeCe and then with Zorro. He zeroes in on me. He glances quickly, with warmth in his big brown eyes, over to Otoña, their mom, then across the plaza to Zachariah, their dad and gives him a quick nod. Extends an arm and waves him over to the veggie table. Then he smiles — back among the self-designated 'community leaders.'

With the little papillae on my tongue, I've licked my fur 'till it shines. I look sleek and clean. I'm ready.

Big Joe takes the Mic. He praises absolutely everyone in a dress or a suit and tie. He calls on all four preachers to make intonements to the Almighty in thanks for blessing this wondrous space and all our good fortune.

Finally, Big Joe pauses. He smiles broadly. "We have all come a long way. This has been an amazing year. Many have contributed to grow healthy vegetables to feed our families and our neighbors. But just a few have gone the extra mile. It is these few who most deserve this honor." I step out from under the table. I nod at Zorro and CeCe.

Joe picks up the plaque. "Our First Annual Community Garden Service Award goes to…"

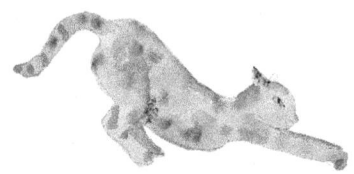

Chapter 2

Abandoned

Let's start at the real beginning — an abandoned lot, abandoned junk, an abandoned cat, *and* an abandoned man.

I'm sitting on a sandy mound one cool fall evening, whiskers out, ears on alert, in the northeast corner of this twenty-acre plot of land. Long ago, some humans had cultivated it, raised crops, then left it to fend for itself. It had been abandoned — for years, maybe for decades, whatever they are.

This particular patch in Phoenix, Arizona, has reverted to desert. The only plants able to survive on their own are a few mesquites and palo verde trees, creosote bushes, and some cacti in a small patch that had been left unplowed — the lone saguaro and a few clusters of prickly pears and cholla on the southwest acre.

Wild animals can survive in an abandoned lot, but they're not abandoned. It's their home. So, rabbits, birds, coyotes and javelina mingle and get along — except for that predator-eat-prey dynamic. The herbivore rabbit may be eating little grasses, and the omnivore coyote may dash in and eat the rabbit.

When people abandoned this field to the wild, they abandoned other junk here too. Over the years rubber tires, toilets, tables, chairs, bags of garbage and even a threadbare couch landed in this northeast corner of the field, far away from the street. Our lot had officially become a "dump."

What was I doing there?

One winter day, some humans drove by on the street south of our plot of desert and threw my mother — their domestic cat *(Felix domesticus)* — out of the car window. Suddenly she became *Felix abandonata* — an abandoned cat.

Being a cat, Mom landed on all four feet. At first she was alone and had to find food for herself. Luckily, the abandoned land was home to field mice, gophers and occasional baby birds that eked out a living on insects, worms and seeds. Mom survived.

Soon, a tom cat, who had been hit by a car on the same nearby street, dragged himself into a damp irrigation ditch at our dump. He lay there for days. He would either heal on his own or die.

He healed. After two days he rose from his ditch, skinny and starving, with a permanent limp. He yawned. He stretched. He did a 'down cat.' His back and legs now loosened up as best they could be, he started to look for food.

To his surprise and delight, a lady cat — a very curious cat — sat within inches, grooming a front paw and staring him in the face. Mom showed him the best places to catch mice. Love bloomed, and after a while Mom gave birth to me!

An abandoned lot also attracts abandoned people. That is how I met Zachariah. And that's when the *community* part of the garden began.

It was a cool evening in the fall. The days were shorter, the nights longer, and the afternoons cooling down. If you're a cat — a warm-blooded mammal — your fur keeps you warm. The snakes — poor ectotherms that they are — need to bury themselves in the ground or some nook to keep warm.

So, early on a chilly evening I am prowling around, slinking stealthily through the underbrush, on the lookout for mice, avoiding the nocturnal great horned owl, when I spot this human. He is tall and skinny, wearing a shabby shirt and torn trousers. He limps toward me and the abandoned couch in the ditch. He puts a paper bag on the ground and hauls the couch out of its ditch. Then he plops down on the couch and retrieves the paper bag. A brown bottle top peeks out of the bag.

He looks really sad. He takes a swig from his bottle and talks in a kind of slurry speech to the weeds and the stars. Curious, I sneak up. He looks over and starts talking to me instead. "Hi, cat," he garbles. "Will you be my friend? I don't have any friends." He burps, then hiccups. "My name's Zach, short for Zachariah. What's yours? I know! I'll call you Sebastian."

At first I retreat under a creosote bush. But there is something comfortably familiar about Zachariah. It seems like someone literally dumped him off — like my mom. Now here's Zach on the couch. He presses up against the cushions for warmth. He looks abandoned too.

He takes another gulp, wipes his mouth, and says, "Don't leave, Sebastian. I need a friend. Nobody wants me. I'm a worthless human being. Will you be my pal?" That's when I nickname him "Sad Zach." I crouch nearby as, exhausted from emptying the brown bottle in the wrinkled bag down his thirsty throat, he lies down and sleeps, all alone, on the abandoned couch.

Chapter 3

Friends

The next thing I know, Sad Zach shows up every night. He's made the couch his home, complete with a ratty rattan side table and a raggedy tarp tied to the trees.

After a few nights, he brings two bags. He unwraps the second one, opens a can, and the smell of tuna fish knocks me over! Did I tell you I am a carnivore? Mice and birds may eat only seeds or gobble up a worm or beetle as well, but frankly, the mice don't always get enough to eat. They are skinny. So, as for my dinner, they leave something to be desired.

Tuna fish! I've never had anything like it, but somehow I know — by instinct — that it's perfect for me! I'm dying to go right up and grab some. But Sad Zach is a human. As a feral cat, I'm wary.

Sad Zach senses my predicament. He whips out a discarded paper plate. He scoops some tuna onto the plate with the lid from the tuna can and shoves it away from him and closer to me. He seems to know I need my space.

Oh My Gosh this smells like manna from heaven! I inch toward the plate. Sad Zach reaches out to pet me. I pull back! He retreats onto a cushion.

"Sorry to scare you, Sebastian. You must be like me — ya don't trust people." He slurs his words. "You're right — can't trust 'em. I forgot. You an' me - we're both abandoned. So, Sebastian, I won't touch you. You can come back and eat the tuna."

Then he does this slow, gentle, staring-gently-at-me blink — his eyes close slowly, then slowly open. I LIKE this. I feel safe and cared for.

But he's human, I'm feral. I still don't trust him.

Plus, he sounds friendly. I don't know if the stuff in his bottle makes his voice soft, but I feel cautiously optimistic. I advance, paw by paw, toward the fish. Sad Zach chills back on his cushion — a sign of respect.

Boy! The tuna is delicious! After a diet of mice and voles, this is great! It's even got Omega-3s in it. I gobble it up.

Chapter 4

Me, Sebastian, The Feral Cat

Time to tell you a little more about me.

First, I am not a tiger — neither a white, Sumatran, Bengal, nor Burmese. I don't live in a jungle. I live in a desert — the Sonoran Desert in the middle of Phoenix, Arizona. And if you were just to observe me creeping around this community garden, you might — mistakenly — think I am domestic. But I'm not.

My mom was abandoned in this lot. My dad barely survived after being hit by a car. For a while, they survived, Unfortunately, a great horned owl snatched my mom. A coyote killed my dad. So I, too, wound up abandoned.

Second, I am not your primped and fussed-over pretty Persian or Siamese who fluffs up on a silk cushion and eats *bonbons* and then has to do her business in a litter box. That kitty never gets to see the true outdoors or live really free — like me.

And they never made a major difference in the creation of a community garden — like me.

I'm just a regular American back-street brindle alley-cat. Brindle means that I have stripes. My stripes are patchy and furry and less defined — quite haphazard, really. But they're all 'earth tones,' like amber, maple, mud, and mahogany, with an occasional dab of tan, sand, and white in between. I like my colors because they match the faces and arms and legs of all the humans who frequent this community garden.

Third, everything I'm going to tell you is true — I swear on a stack of field mice. Although — it is true from *my* point of view. That means you might not see it the same way. But I'm sure you can reach across the species divide for just a short time, while I tell you what I know about *this* community garden.

Aside from the sun and rain, the night and day, winter and summer, a community garden needs air, water, good dirt, insects, microbes, and animals. That includes you *(Homo sapiens)* and me (*Felix catus* or *Felix domesticus*). Without all of us, it ain't gonna happen.

In the morning I finally wake up. Sad Zach is gone. Has he abandoned me?

No! He returns the next night, with two more sacks — a bottle for him, and another can of tuna for me! This routine continues. We're no longer abandoned. We're friends.

Chapter 5

Sad Zach's Story

One evening, after a few tipples from his bottle (I've polished off my share of tuna), Sad Zach opens up. "Sebastian, I guess you should know. I'm a rotten human being. I've done bad things. I was in the war. Plus I'm an ex-felon. I did two years for assaulting my wife — my beloved Otoña" *(I wonder who that is)* "who I've known from when we were kids. I'd never do anything to hurt her — but I did.

"We went to grammar and high school together. I think we loved each other from the git-go. I wanted us to go to the university. I would become an art teacher — did I tell you I was an artist? And she'd become a biologist, or something like that.

"But we got married, and the kids came along, and we had to get jobs. We went to community college and worked part-time. Then I signed up for the Army — it paid a lot better. Before you know it, you're in Afghanistan, fighting a war that you're not sure anyone knows what it's about. She got through community college and became a teacher's aide at a local school — not great pay, but a schedule to match the kids' school time."

Zach takes another big swig — my first lesson that humans can wind themselves up and just talk on and on. Then he resumes his tale of woe.

"When I got back, I had horrible PTSD from the war. That's Post Traumatic Stress Disorder. You can get PTSD when something awful happens in your life. It's pretty common in war. For me, there were two things.

First, I'll never forgive myself for the number of times I used my automatic rifle. The truth is, we killed a lot of people — the 'enemy' and others — sometimes moms and children. Politicians may call it 'collateral damage', but it's wrong! And Sebastian, you don't want to see dead people. Trust me."

Sad Zach takes a break. He uses a dirty rag to wipe his eyes. He breathes in and out, in and out.

"And then the other side — we call them the enemy — would plant IEDs — Improvised Explosive Devices, like homemade bombs — near the road. One time our jeep hit a buried IED and blew up. Two of my buddies were killed. Me and my other buddy were wounded. My best friend lost both his legs. I kept mine, but that's why I have this permanent limp. I have nightmares thinking about it."

Sad Zach stops, shakes his head, then his whole body, like he is trying to get something dirty off him.

"When I came home, I couldn't get the noise, and the shock of the IED, out of my head. At the slightest surprise I'd react. Sometimes I'd just turn around and swat whatever — or whoever — had come up behind me. Other times, something the kids or 'Toña said would set me off in a rage. I'd freak out. She tried to get me to go to the Veterans' Administration for counseling or meds, but I'd have none of it. I was tough!

"Then one afternoon — I'm so ashamed I could die — when the kids and her had all come home from school, they were squabbling about what to have for dinner. A door slammed. I got triggered. I grabbed 'Toña — my wife, the girl I had loved since I was a kid — and threw her up against that door. The doorknob jabbed into her back and broke two ribs. Almost punctured a lung! Zorro called 911. He was only ten years old. The cops came. They took me to jail and her to the hospital. And the kids saw everything.

"Bottom line — she took out an Order of Protection to keep me away from her and the kids, and I was convicted of assault and spent two years in prison. I tell ya, Sebastian, if you don't have PTSD from the war, you'll get it prison. It crushed me.

"But I got out. 'Toña was notified of my release and took out another Order of Protection. I don't blame her. I'm a no-good, rotten, low-down piece of garbage. And, with a felony record, I can't find a place to live or get a job. So I've made my home here on the couch under the palo verdes, as far from the street as I can get so the neighbors won't see me. I'm a homeless bum."

He stops talking for a minute to slug down more from his bottle. I hope it's the end, but no.

"Sebastian, I don't want to be rotten. I want to be with her again. I want to be with my kids again. Soon they'll become teenagers. I've been gone from their lives for the most of five years, and they've lost so much. I want to be a decent human being and turn my life around. Only I don't know how." He grabs a filthy rag, blows his nose in it and wipes his eyes again. "Sebastian, you are my only friend in the world."

Thank goodness, he stops talking. I don't know what all his words mean. But I can tell from the way he falls back against the pillows and lets his hands drop to the side (except for keeping the bottle-in-the-bag upright) that he is spent. He's a very broken man.

But for me, he's been a life-saver. Before him, I was alone. I had to feed on skinny mice and baby birds. Since Sad Zach appeared, it's been tuna paradise. Sad Zach may think he's awful. But to me he's good company. He feeds me. He treats me like a pal, and he's comfortable to snuggle against — as long as he doesn't know it.

Sad Zach is worn out. We're both tired. He stretches out on the lumpy couch. Soon, he's out like a light.

After he nods off, I hop lightly onto the couch — he doesn't even know I'm there — and take a whiff. He smells of sweat, tears, dirt, somethings you humans call "booze" and "fast food," and maybe other stuff too. Not bad, to a cat. I decide to nap as well — nestled cozily within the curve of the back of his knees.

This routine — two paper bags, food, and curling up by his backside — goes on for many months. Sad Zach has made this abandoned lot his home. The days get shorter, the nights longer. The moon comes, fills a full circle, shrinks to a sliver, and disappears — then starts again as a new sliver. The days become longer. Zach shows up at dusk, and we compare notes until he sleeps. It's almost as if we're family.

But all that is about to end.

Chapter 6

The Flood

It's a late day in May — exactly a year ago, according to the human timetable. The daytime weather has turned hot, so I have crawled into a secluded, dry, dark space in which a cat can safely hide, chill out, spy, and sleep — a 12" concrete irrigation pipe from some past era when this whole abandoned field had been a garden.

Suddenly…

Trickle, trickle, gurgle, gurgle, — SPLOOOSH! A blast of water spurts forth through my 12" bedroom! Suddenly, gallons of water gush out of the pipe, hurling me twenty feet down the ditch until I crash into a berm — a ridge between the ditches where the water actually flows. I land with a THUNK!

I'm thoroughly drenched, bruised, and fighting for my life. This is awful! We cats hate water. By that I mean getting wet — which is way different than having a drink. I let out a caterwaul — a cat's double-barreled way of saying "That's awful!"

I recover from the blast, twist myself back upright, cough a few times and dash over to high ground under a mesquite tree. I lick myself dry — that sounds strange, doesn't it? A wet tongue on wetter fur. But I use that rough 'wet' tongue of mine to get the water off and let me 'dry off.'

That's when I notice, back behind that flood of water coming through the pipe, a group of humans clapping their hands as if a miracle had occurred. I am so appalled at this water blast that I yowl. I screech. I hiss. The humans stop clapping.

Suddenly the big guy — I quickly learn that he's Big Joe — spots me. He gives me the stare, — like, "Whaddya mean, hissing at the water, ya dumb cat? And what are you doing here, anyway?"

But then he says, "Wait a minute. You're trying to tell me something! I get it — we just flushed you out of your hiding place. Sorry, cat. Catch ya later…"

So, just a year ago, the community garden began.

Chapter 7

Not Identical Twins!

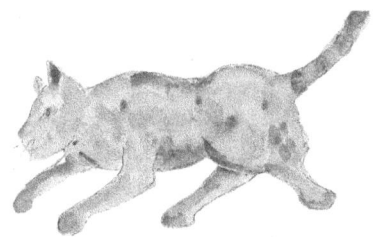

The flood that swooshed me out of bed has two results — one bad, the other good.

The bad part — I mean really bad — is that Zach disappears. He no longer makes his home in the abandoned lot. For me, there's no more tuna, no more friend on the futon. I was sure I had been left in the lurch, that Sad Zach had abandoned me.

But the good part is the arrival of Zorro and CeCe, the fraternal twins who come to the garden after the flood with their mom, Otoña. They first arrive early in June. Then they show up only a few times during the summer. It's really hot! I spend a lot of time seeking shelter — sometimes under the couch. I hope Zach will return, but it just does not happen. I have to scrounge for mice and voles.

The place gets busy despite the hot weather. Within days after the big flood, people started swarming all over our dump. They pluck weeds and scatter mulch, plow pathways and repair pipes. A guy with a cowboy hat, who they call Backhoe, sits atop a tractor and shoves the dead tires and barbed wire down an old dirt road. He dumps everything into a waiting truck that hauls away trash. He discreetly leaves Sad Zach's lumpy couch alone, hidden among some palo verdes.

In June, Backhoe plows open a 'plaza'-type area near the street that separates the garden from a senior housing project — whatever that is. Ike, Tiger and Leo — who have become Big Joe's right-and-left-hand lieutenants, set poles in the ground and run tarps from one pole top to another. Ike runs the irrigation system, Tiger is the master farmer, and Leo coordinates volunteers. All three help set up the shady pavilion.

It's July, hot as a frying pan, and they've completed the plaza. Yay! In August they plough a parking lot and throw gravel on it. September brings seats and tables where various vendors start selling their stuff — vegetables, seeds, and honey. And all this time — no Zachariah.

September also brings CeCe and Zorro — for good.

"Don't call me his twin sister," CeCe snaps at her mom. "He makes a mess with his wild art. He does that stupid hip hop, like he has ants in his pants. We are NOT twins!" She seems to have her nose out of joint, and I haven't even caught a lizard.

"You're fraternal twins, Cecilia" says the mom, Otoña. She speaks in a tired voice that begs for cooperation. "You are not identical; anyone can see that. Calm down!

But you're both smart, you're both good-looking, and"— she pauses to give them her 'look' — "you both know that I need you to help me weed before we plant. Sometimes I simply need your help." She stops, swallows. I see from how her shoulders droop that she has a huge sadness in her. Even with her two kids there, she seems lonely.

"Well, we could look for Dad, Mom. He's out of prison now, isn't he?" demands CeCe.

Zorro adds, "Yeah, he got violent sometimes, but he wasn't all bad. He was OK before the war."

"He could sometimes really be fun!" says CeCe, to top her brother's thought.

"Please, let's not argue," sighs Otoña. "It's not that simple. He's a changed man. You can't pretend it was all fun and games." She breaks off the conversation and runs her fingers through her hair, anxious and tired. I'd say she's worked a full day before she's even arrived at the garden.

"Well, I'm tired of working with *women*!" complains Zorro, the tall dark handsome brother who seems as much out of sorts as his twin sister. "I'm way too old to hang around with her and — my *mother*." He grabs a shovel and thrusts it into a ditch.

"Oh, come on," says Otoña. You're the same age. You're twins."

"No, I'm fifteen minutes older! You told me so. You said I arrived earlier and then she took her time getting born."

Well, I guess that does make him the older brother, but they're from the same litter. I don't understand the fuss.

"If he won't help, I won't either," snaps CeCe. She is not going to be outdone by Zorro.

"One thing for sure," says Otoña, "You both sure are feisty. But please, just help me for ten minutes with the weeding, and then you can wander around the garden. Don't go too far — there's food. I think Theodora (Mrs. Big Joe) is laying out a delicious spread."

That piques their interest. Since their dad was sentenced to two years in prison, and with him not being around after his release, plus with Mom on her own and working a job full-time at their local school, home cooking has become monotonous, with pre-packaged mac 'n cheese, burritos, or popcorn.

So they dig weeds out of a ditch and a few berms and grudgingly follow Mom over to the pavilion.

Who is this 'Joe' guy anyway? And besides, he's a grown up. Why do we have to listen to him? I can feel CeCe and Zorro thinking the same thought just by how they slouch. They do seem to be twins — at least in how they feel about helping Mom and listening to Joe — the guy who heard my caterwaul.

Some powerful aromas waft our way. Long before we arrive on the packed dirt plaza, Theodora's dishes draw my attention. To me, something smells like meat for a cat. She announces, "Come and get it! Grilled chicken, fresh veggies, potatoes, and salad!"

Everyone lines up fast. Apparently Theodora has a rep for good food. I'm sure the meat is something I'd like to sink my teeth into.

But all the food is in large metal containers high on tables, out of cat-reach — at least with a group of humans standing watch. I crouch under a creosote bush, tail waving to and fro, stalking accidental drops, trying to figure out my next move. The humans take all the chicken — and at the end of the day they leave. I'm left to hunt on my own.

Chapter 8

Saturday School #1
You're All Welcome Here!

The next Saturday starts early for the humans — about 8:00 a.m.

A circle forms in the middle of the plaza. Big Joe is clearly the ringleader. He's big, and his voice is big, and people seem to think he's 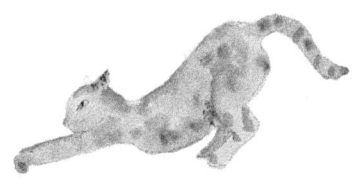 somebody. So he starts what will soon become a regular Saturday School routine.

I hide under a table to spy.

Joe starts with stretches — hands touch the sky, then a big bend into 'down cat,' after which they all rotate their upper halves around — first to the left, then to the right. Even Zorro and CeCe have joined the circle to wriggle and writhe — at opposite sides of the circle, as far from each other as they can be, and still be part of Joe's entourage.

Soon Big Joe launches into his speech. He calls out several other folks by what they're in control of — Backhoe (who drives the backhoe), Ike the Irrigator, Tiger, Leo, Latifa the Beekeeper, Dirt-maker Darlene, and a few old guys like Geronimo and Hurricane, the music man. Joe greets them all. "And last but not least, my better half, Theodora, who is responsible for another wonderful buffet lunch today." At the mention of Theodora and lunch, a huge cheer goes up.

"You notice that some of us are old, some are young, some dark, some light, some speak with a kind of accent. A few of us don't even speak English. Some of us are from here. Some — like my friend the Asian Tiger *(he's clearly a human, not a tiger)* — have recently arrived from other countries. But we're all here to work in the garden.

We're working to make our lives better and to bring healthy food to our families and our community. No matter what your race, your religion, or even if you have no religion — you're all welcome here. Doesn't matter what school you went to, or if you went to school. Doesn't matter if you spent time inside" — he pauses and looks at Ike and Geronimo — "you are all welcome here."

Everyone claps. Everyone in the circle seems to feel welcome here.

But I wonder, *"Where is Sad Zach? Is he welcome? Why isn't he part of the garden? As far as I know, he's the best part of our community. Where did he go?"*

Then Zorro spots me under the table. "Hey, a cat!" All heads turn in my direction. Someone cries out, "A feral cat!" CeCe runs toward my table — but I'm spooked. I vanish — for now.

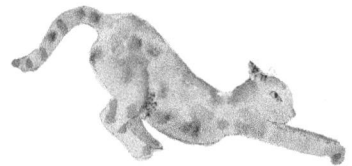

Chapter 9

To Plan or Not to Plan

It's still September. How do I know? I hear the ringleaders — Big Joe, Darlene, and the regulars — talking about how it's September and how they need to plan what to plant, and when. Some are super-organized; others seem more spontaneous.

Me? I have a plan. I'm prowling near the hay bales because there are mounds and holes in the ground that may belong to mice, voles or prairie dogs.

I am definitely in the planning mode. I creep kinda low, nose close to something I just bet is a vole hole, sniffing for clues of recent presence — a fresh scent. No luck at hole #1, so I creep over a mound and around some weeds to hole #2, where I poke my nose again.

Just then, I feel the ground reverberate with the sound of many human feet heading my way.

Spontaneously, the vole in that hole pops out to flee the onslaught. And since I planned so well, I catch it and lay right on the spot, to chow down.

Meanwhile, the humans park themselves on the cluster of hay bales.

At first, the conversation is a veritable free-for-all, several people speaking at once, talking over and interrupting each other. I watch. I try to give them the "I'm the one in charge here" cat stare, but they ignore me.

One says, "We have to honor the ancient Native American tradition of the 'Three Sisters' — planting corn, beans and squash together."

"Whyz zat?" asks a cynic.

"Because," pontificates the original speaker, "the corn stalk grows tall, the beans then grow and curl around the corn stalk, and the squash leaves cover and protect the young bean plant."

"Sounds great," interrupts an old-timer, "but you've got your seasons wrong. It's already late September. Even in our zone, zone #9, with the warmest weather, Corn and squash need at least three months to grow. The days are getting shorter. December will be here, and the plants could catch a frost. We need to plant them in late January."

"Well, I'm going to plant the three sisters," argues CeCe. "Those Native Americans knew what they were doing." She's sure the old-timer doesn't know what he's talking about.

"I'm going to plant chard and kale," insists a lady with long braids, a long skirt, and a long tunic. "I'm going with winter crops." She gets a smug look on her face, like a Mrs. Know-it-All.

Darlene the dirt-buster (you'll get to know her better soon) rings a cow-bell to shut up all the humans. "You're right about needing a longer growing season for some crops," she tells them. But we all have different patches. The only people who need to agree are the ones working in the same little garden. Choose for yourself, and let's see what makes it and what doesn't."

"Hear, hear," cry a few of the fellows who occupy the back row.

"*I'm* just planting prickly pear for jelly," says a lady with black hair. "I'm going to harvest the buds for jelly. Prickly pear cactus can survive the winter, so it doesn't matter when I plant."

"I'm going to plant an orange tree!" declares Zorro. "I love oranges."

Otoña looks at both her children. Until the planning session neither one had expressed any interest in planting anything. Quietly, she decides to let them try what they want, suspecting that there may be lessons to learn.

A man nearby mumbles quietly to himself, "I'm just planting blue agave." He makes sure only his buddy can hear him — except for me with my very sharp cat ears. The buddy chuckles a conspiratorial chuckle. *I wonder what that's all about.*

Latifa adds her two bits. "I'm a big fan of choice," she says. "Why don't we all just do what we think is best in our own plot? We can see what turns out better and when things come ripe. Then we can share our knowledge as we go along."

Amazingly, there's a huge group sigh of relief. Everyone gives her a hand-clap, and they all disperse to their own little garden patches. To me, it looks like some are making a plan, others not so much. Meanwhile, a second vole scooting unplanned out of a nearby mulch pile fits nicely into my plan — lunch.

Chapter 10

The Dirt on Dirt

It's October. The weather is cooler, and people start planting. Darlene and Latifa have partnered up to construct a chicken coop. Zorro helps Backhoe dig post holes to secure the fence. Leo brings along several teenagers he calls his "Juvies" to help with the post-hole digging, plus running fence wire along the posts. There is a lot to do on this lot.

Inside the chicken coop, CeCe helps build nests for the hens to lay their eggs. Next to the fence, away from the henhouse, Darlene has started to assemble the makings of a compost heap.

Nearby, Latifa has set up several boxes that serve as hives for the European honeybees who will both fly out to pollinate needy vegetables and produce honey in their hives.

Otoña comes over to the coop from tilling her garden. 'Otoña' is a Spanish word for 'Autumn,' and it also means 'harvest.' That makes sense. 'Toña has a 'green thumb'. It's not really green. It just means she has a way with making plants grow. She wears rubber gloves to help Darlene blend the food waste and the discarded cardboard into a disgusting mess. She then sprays water all over the pile to putrefy it and make it look — and smell — like rotting slop.

I don't understand the attraction. You combine two types of garbage — gloppy garbage at that —, soak it with hose water, and bingo! It's supposed, magically, to become enriched soil for plants. Just smells like garbage to me. But — it does attract mice and voles. That's a plus — maybe I'll catch dinner.

CeCe stops to wrinkle her nose and sneeze at the smell. Zorro grabs a clod of gook and chucks it at a chicken, who scampers out of reach. He scrunches up another clod — In his bare hands. "CeeC, catch!" he yells, tossing it at her head.

Just now, Big Joe breezes in. "Put that DOWN, Zorro! No food fights. This is *not* the school cafeteria." Too late. Luckily, CeCe ducks and it misses its mark, splotching the side of the henhouse instead. Joe adds, "Listen up! Darlene is the Queen of Dirt. Let's go over to the classroom and she can give y'all the real scoop on soil."

So Zorro, CeCe and the other kids at the garden plop themselves onto the hay bales scattered around the outdoors 'classroom'— a space where you can sit, listen and share. Darlene begins her rap on refuse.

I slink over and hide inside a pomegranate bush. Something catches my eye — I don't see much color, but I can spot a moving mouse at dusk. I see a shifting shadow pretty far to the north, beyond the mulberry tree. Sad Zach stands about twenty berms away — peeking surreptitiously at Darlene's demo. *What's he doing here during the daytime? Where has he been? Why didn't he bring me any tuna? And why doesn't he join the action?*

Darlene takes a magic marker and draws a big black circle on the white-board. "All of life is a circle," she says. "And dirt is a very important part of that circle. Sometimes I call it the 'circle of life'.

"Let's start with the food you eat. We'll end with food too. So, here is our food." She draws a solid orange carrot at the top of the circle — like at 12:00 noon. Next" — she arcs her marker clockwise to about 3:15 o'clock on the circle — "the left-overs land in the compost pile, along with other things that can break down into soil again, like cardboard egg containers, some regular dirt, and even stuff like chicken and duck poop."

Chortles and giggles stop the show.

"No, really," she says. "The poop — like chicken and duck droppings over at the chicken coop or guano from bats — carry nutrients for the dirt. However, poop from humans and most other carnivore mammals is *not* good for the garden." She puts on a stinky-face way worse than CeCe's. "Do not ask why. Just trust me."

She paints green lettuce and brown cardboard with her dry markers. "You need a balance of what you stir into the compost-soon-to-be-soil," she explains. "You need green stuff — like soggy lettuce and grass clippings — and brown stuff — like dead leaves, sawdust and cardboard. It needn't be exactly brown or exactly green, or precisely fifty-fifty, but balance is good. Soil needs a variety of vitamins and minerals, and the different materials make for a balance. Plus," she adds, "the different organisms that break down the compost are attracted to the different materials in the compost. There are even different stages of decomposition — some hotter, some cooler, that attract the different organisms."

I'm about to curl up under a broken crate for a daytime nap — to a feral cat, this is so-o-o-o boring. I need to be ready for my crepuscular food searches. But Zorro interrupts. "What's an organism?"

Then CeCe pipes up, "And what's fifty-fifty, and why does it matter?"

"Good questions," says Darlene. "Let's take 'organism' first. Did you know that each one of us is a separate organism?"

Everyone looks confused. I am.

"Maybe the best way to say it is that an organism is a form of life considered as a self-contained entity — including any individual animal, plant, person, or even a fungus."

Everyone nods, like they know what she means. I sure don't. She goes on, skipping '50-50' for now. "Can anyone give me an example of a fungus?"

CeCe wondered, "A mushroom? We saw some in our back yard."

"Yes! But just to be safe, do not eat, or even touch, a mushroom you see in the garden, or in the wild. Some are edible and delicious. But others are poisonous and can kill you. Let the experts decide."

Toña makes a mental note to dig up and toss the mushrooms in the yard at home.

Darlene picks up a piece of dark rotting cardboard she has captured from the compost heap. "Back to our pile of compost," she continues. "Do you see these tiny white squiggles on the cardboard?"

Eager to mess with the junk, Zorro touches one. "Yew. It's gooey!"

"It's a fungus. Plus the bunch of them that you see along this cardboard. The plural of one fungus is fungi. 'Fun Guy,' get it?"

CeCe laughs. And, since his sister does laugh, Zorro does not.

"That's right!" Darlene's on a roll. "It's tiny little fungi that decompose — that means they eat — the cardboard into even smaller matter. And guess what? Some fungi are attracted to the brown stuff in the compost while other fungi are attracted to the greens." Darlene emphasizes the sound of the word — 'fun guy' each time she says it, like she's having fun.

Zorro does not correct her to say that the plural of 'fun guy' is 'fun guys,' because he gets it — fungi is already the plural of fungus. Darlene swings her arm holding the black marker down to 6:30 o'clock on the bottom of the circle, where she draws squiggles. "Earthworms also help biodegrade and change the compost back into good dirt," she says. "Not just any worm, but those brownish-pink ones you've seen in the soil. They eat various matter and — *here we go again* — poop it out into smaller particles of dirt."

She finally swings her marker over to 9:45 o'clock on the circle and draws a few little seeds and seedlings. "Once all the compost has turned into a nutritious batch of soil, we plant the seeds, we water them, and they grow into the vegetables that we pick for dinner."

"Like beans, corn, tomatoes — and carrots," adds CeCe. "I see the whole circle. You're right, Darlene. It is a circle of life. From live carrot to garbage to fungi to compost, to seeds and back to carrots."

"Darlene smiles. "And this is just scratching the surface. We need to understand even more if we want the totally 'down and dirty' version." She laughs.

Well, duh! Dirt is dirty. Even I know that. This cat's boring is the human lady's funny.

Chapter 11

CeCe's Voice

CeCe quietly heads west. She passes a group of garden volunteers tending to spinach, dill and turnips. She follows a series of narrow wood-chip paths that lead from one individual garden to another and then connect to a wider wood-chip road where Backhoe can drive the tractor. She meanders past an "incubator" garden where some of the oldest of the garden ladies are fussing over raised beds — and not hurting their backs. They tend the youngest of seedlings before moving them to the growing garden.

I wish Mom wasn't so sad all the time. It makes her bossy. It was more fun being around her back before Dad — CeCe tries to stuff her feelings back inside somewhere, but they surface anyway. *That day he threw her against the door was horrible. Horrible! But he wasn't always like that.* She trips on some crates left in the road and stumbles, falling against a 500-gallon water storage tank. *She's so wrapped up in herself, she doesn't understand me at all. Nobody does.*

Regaining her balance, she breathes deeply and wipes her eyes on a shirttail. *Maybe if I can find some animals to look at...*

Arriving at the botanical volunteer patch, she squats on her haunches as a night lizard perches on a rock doing push-ups. "You'll make a fine addition to my terrarium," she whispers, then reaches out to grab Mrs. Lizard with both hands.

Suddenly, it's as if a hand grips her shoulder. She thinks she hears a murmur — "CeCe, leave the lizard alone. This is her home."

Startled, CeCe looks around. But there's no one to be seen except the willow tree and its shadows. What just happened? *Did I really feel a hand on my shoulder? Did I really hear a voice?* She wants to catch Mrs. Lizard, but she knows it's wrong to take her away from her habitat and put her in a cage. It's as if the 'voice' is her conscience. Unsettled, CeCe sits quietly, studying the lizard. She begins to notice the movements, the darting, the flicking of the tongue and tail. *Observation does teach more than snatching!* She smiles. A sense of calm settles in.

After a few minutes, Botanical Barb comes over. She's been working on this plot alone and is glad for the young company. "Hi, I'm Barb," she says. "What's your name?"

"Hi, I'm CeCe. My mom's Otoña, over there in our garden." She hops up and waves her arm in the general direction from whence she arrived.

"Great, I know your mom," says Barb. "Do you want to hang out here a little? I'm just getting started on my garden. I sure would like the company. I see you spotted the lizard. There'll be other creatures to see if you just sit quietly."

As CeCe follows Barb, I trot back along the wood-chip roadway bordered by recently planted plum, orange and lemon trees and track down Zorro, who has also skipped out on Mom's "soil enrichment" project and has found the muralist.

Chapter 12

Zorro's Muse

Tubes of acrylic paints clutter the bed of Wiley's pickup truck. Wiley is the garden muralist. He's gotten the green light (as if I could tell the difference) to paint a running mural on the east wall bordering the garden from north to south, chronicling the story of the garden as it grows — by acres, vegetables, trees, irrigation (ugh!), and people.

Today he designs a section where kids are playing — running, swinging, splashing. Zorro arrives and, in an off-hand sort of way, says, "Hi. Are you the artist? I'm Zorro."

"Wiley here. Nice to meet you." They bump fists. Wiley's paint-covered knuckles spread color onto Zorro's. I notice how Zorro seems comfortable here and how Wiley picks up on the 'wanna-be-artist' vibe. Both look down at their multicolored hands and laugh. I don't see what's so funny, but I like their body language — friendship.

The muralist suddenly seems to have a bright idea. "Hey, Zorro, would you mind posing for me? I need a live model. Grab hold of that rope in the palo verde tree branch and swing on it. I'd like to put you in the mural."

"Sure!" Zorro grabs the rope with a big knot, walks it back as far as he can, and then, grabbing the knot, runs and sets himself in motion. He's swinging!

He's not the only one moving. Out of the corner of my clever cat's eye, I spot a shadow among the willow and mesquite trees. Someone's there, to the north, but the low-slung branches block my view.

Suddenly Zorro's hands slip off the rope. He falls into an irrigation ditch full of water with a huge splash! He's soaking wet. The shadow starts to move.

Zorro jumps up with a laugh. He's unhurt. "Hey, Wiley, can I do that again? That was fun," he asks as he grabs the rope again.

The shadow disappears in the distance.

"You better not, kid," warns Wiley, glancing to the north, then throwing him a large dirty towel to dry himself off with. "Your mom will have a conniption fit. But help me choose the colors for this segment. I want to paint you swinging, and splashing, while I remember what that big splash looks like."

Zorro wraps a second towel around himself to get warm. He squeezes white, brown, green, blue, and yellow blobs onto a big palette as Wiley paints a boy swinging above the irrigation ditch into the mural.

While the shadow has receded from view, I detect a lingering odor of brown bags. Meanwhile, these two art fiends are busy painting in color — which I apparently do not appreciate — and showing movement, which looks like loads of fun.

Chapter 13

The Road Map

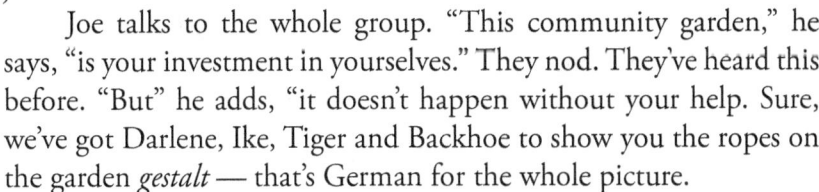

Early the next morning, Darlene, Ike, Tiger and Backhoe cluster around Joe near the tool shed by the mural. I've seen them all before. This time it's different. Sad Zach has joined them.

A troop of older has-beens and younger maybe wannabes shuffle up to the leadership team. They seem to be seeking something. It's not just about the weeds.

Joe talks to the whole group. "This community garden," he says, "is your investment in yourselves." They nod. They've heard this before. "But" he adds, "it doesn't happen without your help. Sure, we've got Darlene, Ike, Tiger and Backhoe to show you the ropes on the garden *gestalt* — that's German for the whole picture.

"But the hard part is making the *community.* It is you guys — each one of you — planning your own road map and working your plan. And it works better if you have a peer mentor."

They all nod, like this is a re-hash of an earlier lesson. "Now, here we're all peers, we're equals," he continues. But some of them don't feel equal. The older men shuffle and cough. The teens stare at their Jordan Air knock-offs.

"Yes, we are," says Joe. "Some of you have been through bad stuff. You may have slipped up. Our old-timer Geronimo, here," he chuckles, "absolutely knows what I'm talking about — don't cha, Geronimo? But I have too. We've all stumbled. It takes hard work to forge a new direction.

"That's why each one of you" — he eyes the teen-agers who hold themselves a little apart from the garden pros — each one of you has a mentor. Each one of you works with Darlene, Tiger, Ike, or Backhoe. Each one of us decides what we want to accomplish — today, this week, this month, this year. We talk with each other about how to do that — what tools we employ, to get the job done, both in the garden *and* as we move along on our own personal path.

"So I want to welcome Zachariah here. He is one of us. Life's been hard on him, and he's made mistakes, but my pal Zach here, he's working his road map." Joe puts an arm around him and asks, "Zachariah, what is one thing you are trying to do each day, to improve your life in this community garden?"

Sad Zach clears his throat. "This is what's key to me. I show up every day and follow your guidance. You folks at the garden help me create a plan that maybe I can work on, and I can succeed at. I focus on trying to do what needs to be done. You're my peer mentors as I try to work the plan. You create hope for me, even when I don't have it myself."

He stops and looks down at some weeds in the dirt. Everyone pauses. For all of them, life has been hard. The garden is a new chance. This is serious stuff.

Then Zach looks back up, glances around the group, and smiles. For some reason, he decides to make a joke. "Turns out, I'm a Dr. Dan fan.'"

All the guys laugh. I don't get it.

"I'm a fan, you're a fan, we're all fans of Dr. Dan's — Super Soda! What I'm saying, guys, is"— he takes a deep breath — "alcohol has not been my friend. It ruined me, it harmed my family, it put me in prison and then out on the street. For a while, after I got out, I was homeless." Another deep breath. "I lived on the crumbling couch here in the garden."

He glances over toward the prickly pear plant. I sit there, cat-eyes on Zach, silently cheering him on. "And if it hadn't been for my friend Sebastian" — he gives me the nod — "I might not have been able to turn that corner. First, being able to talk to my nonjudgmental friend. Next, to join a Veteran's AA group. That's Alcoholics Anonymous. And then to meet up with Big Joe here," — he bumps shoulders with Joe — "and plot out my road map. Sebastian was my first friend. He accepted me unconditionally and let me talk it out. We meditated together, Sebastian and me. He became my *community*. We're like family now, aren't we, Sebastian?"

I trot over and rub up against his trousers. "Meow." *I am glad you're back, Sad Zach. But I'd still like some tuna.*

Chapter 14

The Birds and the Bees

One day early in November there's a catastrophe. It has to do with the birds and the bees — or more specifically, the bees and the chickens and the muscovy duck. I do my best to save the day, and CeCe runs for help, but by the time the adults arrive, it's too late.

Latifa the honeybee lady has placed her beehive boxes away from the actual gardens where folks grow their vegetables, and near the compost heap. There, those fun fungi are nibbling on soggy cardboard to decompose it and mix it with the dirt and veggie leftovers. The composting process will continue that great circle of life, turning rot into mulch, where seeds can grow into sugar-snap peas, beets and peppers.

So the bees are neighbors with the chickens and ducks — as in very close proximity. It seems to be a good idea — away from most human traffic, and away from me. Bees sting.

I like being around Latifa, though. When she gets honey from her bees, all outfitted from head to toe with a screen hat, she works with a calm sense of purpose. As a cat, I find that she and I can move pretty comfortably among the bees, because we can be slow, calm and quiet. We don't bother them — and they don't bother us.

Why do they have bees at all in the garden? Because they are pollinators. Pollen is that stuff in plants that ultimately helps make new flowers, fruits and vegetables. Pollen needs to move from one flower to another, in order to pollinate the next one. And pollen moves only by wind or by insects — like bees. Bees fly around on their little bee wings to the flowers of all sorts of plants — and they get the pollen all over themselves, especially their legs or abdomen, and then they take the pollen to the next plant and the two pollen parts of the plant mix up.

Flowers make more flowers and fruits. With vegetables like zucchini, the mix of pollen from one zucchini flower to the other makes possible the actual zucchini vegetable. You gotta have somebody — like the wind or a bee — to pollinate the two flowers together.

This is really important! If the bees pollinate the crops, veggies grow, and people have food. The circle of life continues. If not, no food for people.

But, more about bees. When I hang around Latifa, she gives me an earful!

Did you know that honeybees live in colonies? When wild, they can live in trees. When "managed" by humans, honeybees can live in bee-boxes called hives. When they fly out to do their pollinator thing, they memorize where their hive is, so they always know where to return. They have stingers to defend themselves. The bees near the compost are "managed" by Latifa and other humans. They live in a wooden beehive box next to the chicken coop and fenced-in yard.

Sounds good, but think about it. The fence keeps the chickens and duck inside. But the bees can fly anywhere. It's a recipe for disaster!

Just as an FYI, there are lots of different kinds of bees. The two you probably know the best are the European Honey bee (*Apis*) and the Golden Northern Bumble Bee *(Bombus)*. Bumble bees can live in abandoned rodent holes in the ground, or they can steal an empty hive from wild honey bees when the queen and some of her loyalists leave to start a new hive. The bumble bees basically get the worker honey bees who are left behind to raise their own bumble bee babies. Bumble bees are also the best bees at pollinating tomatoes, bell peppers and eggplants. Don't ask why — I have no idea. And if you like to think of them as competing with honey bees, bumble bees do better at pollinating plants in a greenhouse. At least that's what Latifa says — as if it matters to me.

Humans often talk about invasive species — plants or animals. Some of them cause harm to the environment. They never mention the honey bee, even though it came from Europe — so both the European people and the European honey bees are "invasive" here in Arizona. Are they good for us here in the community garden? Yes — because Zachariah brings me tuna fish! And because people grow all the vegetables. Those invasive European honey bees, as good pollinators, are the only bee in North America to make harvestable honey. That's what Latifa has begun to collect. So they're good for the environment too.

Not that I care — I prefer meat and fish.

But there are two brands of European bees — the mild Italian bees, and the more aggressive Africanized honey bees. Watch out — here comes trouble!

On this particular morning I'm sneaking over toward the chicken coop. With all that garbage — I mean compost — mice and voles fulfill their role as part of the circle of life in the food chain — as scavengers eating grubs and insects, and then becoming prey. They scurry into the compost pile — and, with luck, on the way out they become a meal for me.

Both the honeybee and the bumble bee will sting you if they get caught in your shirt or — with honey bees — if you disturb their hive for no good reason. That I can understand. I would hiss and claw at an invader — remember the water flooding my irrigation-pipe bedroom?

CeCe has drifted over to the henhouse, standing outside. She tosses some stale bread over the wire fence into the coop. The chickens and duck waddle and scurry quickly over toward the breadcrumbs to snatch a snack.

Africanized bees will set out to 'defend' their hive way faster than the Italian honey bees. I think we've found ourselves stuck with the Africanized bees. Because suddenly — maybe because the chickens and duck scoot across their yard — those honeybees swarm out of their honeybee box and start dive-bombing the chickens and the duck. They make an angry buzz, buzz, buzzzzzz like I've never heard before! And some of the bees attack the duck. I can't believe what I see. One bee has landed on the Muscovy duck's eyelid and stung her right in the eyeball and made her blind!

I let out a hiss as loud as I could and dive under a bunch of brambles! Something's wrong!

CeCe hears me hiss and realizes the bees are swarming! She screams. Then she dashes like mad over to the tarps where the grown-ups are schmoozing. She yells, "There's a bee attack on the chickens! Help!!"

Latifa is nowhere to be found. It's her day off. People panic — no one knows what to do. Hearing the commotion, Otoña runs over from her little garden. She yells, "Where's the smoke pot?"

It's in the storage shed. Toña rushes in, grabs the pot, lights it, and smoke starts pouring out. She sprints right over to where the trouble began — the coop. Ten feet from the fence she slows down, aghast. Two chickens and the duck are lying on the ground. The bees have stung them a gazillion times. And since bees usually die after they sting, there are little dead bee bodies all over the ground as well.

Toña rolls down her sleeves to her wrists, drops a bandana over her head and neck while still trying to see what she's doing, and walks slowly forward. She swings the smoke-pot. One step, then another, 'till she reaches the chicken-wire fence.

The bees hover close to her face, sensing her breath. She uses her "don't want no trouble" voice and opens the gate to the pen. She holds the smoke-pot high like a candle or lantern — at about her eye-level — where the bees swarm. They hover around her. Then, slowly and steadily, they reverse course. Finally, they retreat, calmed or confused by the smoke, back inside their hive box.

But the damage has been done. Big Joe and Tiger appear on the scene — after it's safe — and pick up the chickens and duck. "We gotta take them to the vet!" yells Joe. He and Tiger run off, duck and hens in their arms, hop into the truck on the street, and split.

Meanwhile, Zorro charges over from the mural to see what the ruckus is all about. Toña tells him, "If it hadn't been for CeCe, we might not have saved any of them. As it is, I think the duck will die."

CeCe adds, "It was the cat. He was hissing at me to get someone. Weren't you, cat?"

I poke my head out. "Meow." I don't think anyone else notices me except Zorro.

And meanwhile, the mice have deserted the compost heap. I go hungry. As I said, the day is a complete disaster!

Chapter 15

Community Garden #101: What Do We Do?

The day after the birds and bees debacle, Big Joe gathers a bunch of folks on the circle of tree stumps next to the hay bales. They have a talk. "We can't have disasters like that again," he says. "We need more order, some improvements, some help. What do y'all suggest?"

Latifa states the obvious. "I should have put someone else in charge when I was gone," she laments. "I am so sorry! If I had shown someone how to handle the bees, that never would have happened. We're lucky that Otoña knew where the smoke pot was and what to do with it."

"Meow." *Aren't you overlooking something? Someone? A girl? A cat??*

Otoña demurs. "No, I was lucky. I'd seen a video. But I wouldn't have acted so fast except for CeCe. She screamed and came running. She knew we needed to help."

CeCe pipes up, "If it hadn't been for the cat I wouldn't have realized it so fast. You let out a warning hiss worse than… !" She tries to come over to the bushes to show me off, but I dive deeper.

"Anyway," Latifa adds, "we need a chain of command and training on how to handle the bees. More than that, I think we need to change out our beehive." Latifa is really upset. She feels guilty. I can smell her anxiety. "Let's have someone look at these bees. I think they've been Africanized. I didn't think so at first. But now I think we need to get ourselves the older, Italian honey bees."

Several folks nod assent and a few agree to meet with Latifa and arrange a session on how to switch out the bees and where to keep the smoke pot, netting, and stuff like that. Step 1.

Big Joe invites others to raise concerns. Crabgrass, one of the juvie wannabes, suggests, "We need to know where to put tools when we're done using them." He has been digging potholes and routing out weeds — like crabgrass. Hence his name. He's right. Step 2.

"Good idea." Big Joe nods to Darlene who starts a list.

"And more music." Zorro is really grooving over by the amps with Hurricane. We're making some progress, here. Step 3.

CeCe adds, "We need bathrooms! When I gotta go, there isn't anywhere to go. I gotta get Mom to drive me home or go to the far side and use the bushes."

Big Joe nods. "You are so right, CeCe. I've seen many a"— He stops, deciding not to go into detail. Step. 4.

Everyone applauds, a lot! I guess humans are fussier about their litter box than we feral cats.

Ike ads his two bits. "I run the irrigation system. We have water, but we don't conserve it. If we could install pipes and drip-hoses"…

I want to hug Ike. Or at least rub against his pants leg. Finally someone gets my point about too much water. Step 5.

A little old lady sitting on a log raises her hand. Quietly, she says, "I have just retired from working in a bank. I'm also on a major charitable fund Board." (*I wonder — is a board of wood the same as a fund board?*) She takes a breath, then adds, "I can talk to some people and get financial help." The biggest step of all — Step 6 — money to get the job done.

Chapter 16

The Shadow Leaves a Trace

Weeks pass. It's December. Many crops have been harvested. The local farmers' market is full of produce. People will enjoy a healthy holiday.

However, CeCe's corn, beans and squash are dead, dead, dead. A killing frost hit many of the summer plants right after Thanksgiving, blackening the large broad squash leaves. The few corn stalks weren't enough for good cross-pollination. The beans started to climb the stalks, but the frost pinched their flower buds. The short days and cold nights proved that the fall growing season was indeed too short.

"It's not fair!" cries CeCe as she surveys the damage. I planted them, I watered them. Mom, stop looking at me. It's not my fault!"

Meanwhile, Zorro learns that his young orange tree won't bear fruit to eat for a few seasons.

Otoña keeps quiet. The kids have enough to feel bad about. Thanksgiving was awkward — again without Dad — and she tried to keep up their spirits by joining with some other garden ladies for a community meal. The diversion worked — everyone was well-fed and had a good time. Some of Otoña's carrots and spinach had been part of the holiday spread. But there was an absence, and CeCe and Zorro felt it.

This Saturday morning, two large envelopes appear on the little bench in Otoña's garden — one marked for CeCe, the other for Zorro. Ribbons adorn them — one red, one green. At least that's what they say. I can't tell colors like that. Christmas has landed.

"What's this? I didn't know mail came to the garden," asks CeCe as she starts tearing open her envelope.

"They don't, silly," answers her non-identical-twin brother. "Someone must have snuck in and put it here." His package is bulkier — almost a box. He, too, starts to rip it open.

"Hold on, wait," warns Otoña, "is there a name of who sent it?"

But she's too late. The envelopes fall to the ground.

A professional artist's sketch pad falls out of each packet. A metal box set of two dozen-colored pencils, plus charcoal and lead black pencils, plus a sharpener and eraser, land on top of CeCe's pad. A note taped to the top of the box says, "To Cecilia. You have a good eye for animals. Mind the science."

Meanwhile, Zorro grabs six bright-colored vials of acrylic paints plus a pack of day-glo markers, as they tumble out of the packet. His message reads, "To Zorro. You know your colors. Master your technique."

Otoña studies the handwriting.

CeCe interrupts whatever thoughts Mom might have had. "Can we keep them? I can't wait to start drawing!"

"How could anyone know what I wanted?" exclaims Zorro. "I watched Mr. Wiley as he was painting the mural, but…"

Otoña sighs. "Just be careful. And take care of your art supplies. These are *very good* quality." She wonders, *Is he here?*

Chapter 17

Christmas In The Garden

It's a chilly, cloudy lonely day here in the garden. I caught a mouse as it left the chicken coop compost heap this morning, so I'm not too hungry. But no humans have come around. Not CeCe. Not Zorro. Not Backhoe or Latifa. Not even Zachariah. I'm beginning to forget about him, since he seems to have forgotten about me.

I wonder where the people are. I check out the parking lot, the tarps, the hay bale outdoor classroom, even the sink by the human bathrooms. *Nada,* nothing, no one. I'm getting used to people, so I feel lonely.

I head over to the crumbling couch on the inside edge of the Healing Garden, which doubles as the Pollinator Garden. Brittle bush, globe mallow, sow thistle, Arizona milkweed, oregano, *hierba buena* (mint), and rosemary bushes all create a well-defined but roomy quiet zone under the canopy of moringa, palo verde and mesquites trees. There is no irrigation at all here. No wonder I love it. Drought-tolerant agave and prickly pear cacti form a dry border around the zone.

Sad Zach usually hangs out here when he's not learning the garden ropes and coaching teenagers on weeds. But he's not here now. I leap soundlessly onto the couch, sniff his stale scent — mostly fast food and sweat. He hasn't been here in weeks. I miss him, even more than the tuna. I'd been getting used to this abandoned human, and now his absence makes me feel more abandoned. I swirl around in a few circles, push my backside up against a pillow, and nap.

Soon, the sound of crunching gravel wakes me. None of my wild neighbors make that much noise. I'm instantly alert.

It's Sad Zach! I'm really glad to see him!

But I've got my pride. *You've been taking me for granted!* I sit up, lick my front paw, give him a blank-stare cat-look.

"Hey, Sebastian, can I share that couch with you?" he asks. Before I can answer he plops down next to me. He has not one, not two, but three containers with him, all fitting into a cardboard tray left over from holding little pots of seedlings.

"Merry Christmas," says Zach. "I got the day off from the halfway house where I've found a place to live, because all the other guys had family visits. I'm not allowed."

Sadly, I understand what this is all about. I give him a semi-welcome, not-quite-forgiving "Meow."

"Anyway, I brought you a Christmas present. Yes I've got tuna, but I have something else. Take a lick." He extracts a can of albacore from one bag, opens it, and sets it on a cushion right next to me. As I light-footedly approach, he takes a container out of the second bag, opens it, and pours some thick white liquid into a dirt-smudged paper bowl. "Extra heavy cream. Try it, my man, I think you'll like it."

I can tell by the smell that I'm going to like it. But I don't want to appear too eager. After nibbling a dainty chunk of tuna, I lick my front paw and stroke my whiskers to clean them up from the fish. Then I delve into the cream.

Wow! Simply delicious! I guess I forgive Sad Zach for all his absences. "Meowwww!"

Then he lifts a huge red cup from his tray that says, 'Dr. Dan' and takes a noisy slurp from a very long straw. "Do you notice the difference, Sebastian? I'm on the wagon." Clearly he's not on a wagon, but he continues. "I don't drink anymore." Of course he is drinking, so I'm not sure what he means. "I've stayed sober since last June.

"Big Joe — I've known him since high school — found me and worked to get me into a half-way house for ex-cons and addicts. He brought me back to the garden to work. I would have come over sooner, but I live at this real house" *(the couch is not real?)* "and, Big Joe keeps me very busy when I'm here. I work in the garden almost every day. Backhoe, Tiger, Ike, and Darlene are schooling me in dirt, water, mulch, and growing vegetables to help the community. Latifa told me to stay away from the beehives, for now. I've started helping train some of the 'Juvies.' I'm even a 'mentor'."

I'm not sure what 'Juvies' are or 'mentor'. "Meow?"

"You know, the teens like Crabgrass and Clodbuster who lean on shovels and haul mulch and don't quite know what to do with themselves. They've been involved in the 'Juvenile Court System.' Seems Big Joe thinks I can be useful because I've made some bad mistakes and can talk with them about how not to do what I did. I've got a long way to go, but coming here almost every day really helps. I know I'm doing something good — for me, for those Juvie kids, and for the community.

"One of our regular projects is pulling out invasive weeds like the stinkweed — aka globe chamomile — the cute, yellow-balled plant that will take over and suck up all the water and starve the native plants, if we don't eliminate it. It's a real predator. It's harmful to everyone's crops in the community garden, so we do a regular sweep of all the individual plots and help keep the damage down. The kids seem to like the feeling that they make a contribution here.

"Sorry I haven't brought you any tuna. I've missed our talks. But I'm working on being a better person." He pauses and takes another huge swig from his enormous jug of Dr. Dan.

"Sebastian, there's a reason for all this. It's not just for me that I'm working on myself. I want to see"... He stops, swallows, starts to talk again and then chokes up.

"Do you know that woman and those two kids who come to the garden? He points over in the direction of Otoña's plot. But no one is here today. "Zorro and Cecilia are my kids."

"Meow?" *Of course I know Otoña, CeCe and Zorro — they're my pals! They're regulars here.*

He suddenly puts his head into his hands. He grabs one of his dirty rags, wipes his eyes and blows his nose.

"Meow-w-w." A low purr. *It's OK, Sad Zach, you're my friend. We're both abandoned, remember?*

"It's Christmas today," he says, "a day when families should be together. They're all together. And I can't be there, because I'm the worst human on the planet.

"Meow?"

"I love her so much, and I love my kids. And I'm not allowed to go near them." He pauses. "They're both gonna be fine artists someday."

So you're the one who gave them the paints and pencils!

"Or she may become some kind of animal or botanical scientist. And he might pick music. Or become an art teacher, like I wanted to be."

I try to make him feel better. "Meow."

He says, "Tell them I love them, OK? I'm trying to manage my anger better — my unpredictable rages. I go to a therapist every week. I meet with a Veterans' peer group from the VA. They all have PTSD. We have the war in common.

"And I try to meditate. Sometimes I'll sit quietly, breathe in and out slowly, focus on my breath, try to keep my mind on beautiful spaces — like this Healing Garden. Would you like to meditate for a while?" He looks out at the plants around us, quiet under a cloudy sky, and closes his eyes. But he's not asleep. He just breathes quietly, in and out, in and out.

I curl up in a circle near him and close my eyes too. I guess you'd call it 'cat meditation.'

After a while, Sad Zach opens his eyes, lets out a long, calm sigh, and stretches his arms and legs. I wake up.

Then he does something he's never done before. He rubs my head gently and tickles a little behind my ears. I've never let anyone do this before. But now I know why he is sad, and he doesn't scare me at all. I lean into his curled fingers. Clearly he needs some love. *I do too.* I let my throat and body rumble gently. "Purr."

"Thanks, Sebastian. That's about the best Christmas present anyone could give me right now."

Chapter 18

Saturday School #2
Martin Luther King Jr. Day

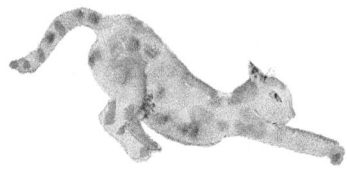

It was quiet for a few weeks after Christmas. It rained, a chill set in, and most folks stayed home. But now it's mid-January. CeCe and Zorro stand across the plaza from each other, holding hands with friends — *not* each other — in the "Saturday School Circle."

Big Joe begins with the usual stretches. Then he launches into his monologue.

"Today," he says, "is Martin Luther King Saturday. We celebrate peace and brotherhood and justice." I wonder, *Do you mean sisterhood and inter-species-hood too?* Joe goes on. "Our Brother Martin was a gift to all of us, leading the way for civil rights for all Americans. He was a great man.

"Not all of us can be Martin. We're not all going to be leaders of a big movement for civil rights.

"But we can all be *like* Martin. We can all strive to be the best at whatever we try to do. If you drive a tractor, you be the best tractor-driver you can be. Just look at Backhoe. People are saying, "There's the best tractor-driver that ever there was." Backhoe turns a deep shade of blush.

"And Darlene makes the best dirt." Supportive laughter accompanies Darlene's modest bow.

You can be a schoolteacher, drive a garbage truck, or grow a community garden. Anywhere you go, it don't matter what you do. City or country, you can do whatever it is, but always try to do the best you can do. Here in the garden, we're here to celebrate all of us doing our best, trying to become better people."

Everybody claps.

"What do you want to be? Speak up."

Some of the boys and girls raise their hands. He calls on them, one by one. "What do you want to be?"

"A doctor." "An electrician." "I don't know." After each one shares their dream, Joe urges the crowd to give that young man — or young woman, or boy, or girl — a round of applause.

CeCe pipes up, "I want to study animals."

Emboldened, Zorro adds, "Someday I'm gonna be an artist. Or a drummer." Everyone in the circle cheers. His pals slap their hands on their thighs, drumming.

Sad Zach stands far off in the distance, hiding in the shadows of the pollinator garden. He has never joined the circle. Now I understand why. But, as volunteers go off in different directions, Big Joe also heads to the northeast. I see them talking. I don't hear any of it. But CeCe asks, "Mom, isn't that...?"

Otoña suddenly spots Sad Zach talking to Big Joe. She looks like she's seen a ghost. "Oh, no!"

"Look, Mom," she pleads, "can't we just move on? I mean, I know he was horrible to you after the war. But I think he's the one who sent our Christmas art supplies. You don't have to see him again, but I want to!" She clomps her arms against her chest in a gesture of "my way or the highway."

Otoña stumbles back, as if she's been punched in the stomach. CeCe has never been this angry, nor this blunt. "It's not that simple, Cecelia," she answers, her voice a tremor. "I don't want you to get hurt. Just stay away from him, honey. Please."

Hmm. *I wonder what Big Joe has in mind as he chats with Zachariah.*

Chapter 19

Water, Water, Everywhere And Not a Drop to Waste

It's late February. A lot keeps happening. Back on Valentine's Day, Big Joe gave a lovey-dovey Saturday School talk, but Sad Zach was still not among the circle. *No wonder he's sad,* I think. But I've progressed to rubbing up against the legs of both Zorro and CeCe. Not their mom. She seems determined to be sad, sort of like — but different than — Sad Zach. She is  virtually always in overdrive, working too hard on her little plot of the garden — like she has to stay busy to keep her mind off something else. Zorro & CeCe don't know my name, but they like having me around. Zorro has brought some cat kibble. It's not as good as Zach's tuna, but it's better than a smelly vole from the compost heap.

Meanwhile, the little old ladies from the senior citizen apartment complex across the street to the south have found the garden. They arrive first thing every Saturday, set up their folding tables and plastic chairs, and they make everyone sign in. They say this is for keeping track of the volunteer hours that some of the non-profits need to know about, so they'll give grant money to keep the garden going.

Theodora has decided that providing a hot lunch on Saturdays should be a regular event, and she enlists several of the retirement ladies to help mix the salads and set up the buffet. When the crowd arrives, everyone moves — and the food disappears — fast.

I don't understand any of the volunteer stuff, much less care, but they go ahead with their tables and pads and pencils anyway. Some of them have noticed me. They've started putting down a plate of cream by one of the tables — a little distance but not too far —

just nice. Not extra thick and heavy, like Sad Zach's, but very good. They call it "Half and Half."

"Meow." *Yes, I do like this, thank you!* I slurp it down. Sometimes one of them, hobbling on her walker, will come over with a refill. "Purr!"

A construction company that the retired bank lady knew about installed permanent block-wall bathrooms just before Christmas — one for guys, one for gals. CeCe is thrilled. There's a sink outside for washing hands. *That's good, but why don't they just lick their skin like I lick my fur? It gets the job done.*

The main improvement is a new "drip" irrigation system, so that more water goes to crops and less of it can splash me. I feel hopeful.

Zorro has started hanging around the art and music men — Wiley the muralist and Hurricane the disc jockey. He carries his sketch pad in a shoulder bag. He's drawing everyone on the move — this kid likes action!

Today, CeCe and her mom are helping a new group of gardeners set up their drip irrigation system. A plumbing company has donated a lot of second-hand, or re-purposed, white plastic pipe. It runs underground from some old 'laterals' and concrete pipes (like my once-upon-a-time bedroom) to each garden.

This new group fits right in — wide brimmed hats to keep off the sun, shorts or overalls with pockets for seeds, a trowel, and work gloves. They flatten the berm-tops and weed the ditches in their little patch of garden. They've even laid black plastic into the ditches between berms to prevent weeds from growing there.

The group is called "The AGC Team," for "All God's Children." Sounds weird, since they all seem to be grown-ups. The 'help-ee' workers are 'developmental' gardeners paired with the 'help-er' volunteers who show them how to plant and fit irrigation hoses together. The help-ers say everything out loud to the help-ees. I guess it's a teaching method. Then, together, they do what they said they would do. They attach the rubber 'holey' drip hose to the end of the PVC pipe that sticks up out of the ground. They lay it out by hand along the length of the berm. Finally they connect the drip hose from the PVC pipe at one end of the berm to another piece of PVC pipe at the other end, and everything stays perfectly in place.

CeCe waves "Hi, Henry" to a grown-up, and she shows him how to lay the hose just right. Henry, it seems, appreciates her guidance. He doesn't speak too clearly, but I recognize a "Tank-ooo" and a smile. CeCe keeps holding the hose until Henry has attached one end of it to the pipe where water comes out, and the other end to the pipe which stops the flow of water. Henry follows her directions to the T. He's smarter than many of the volunteers, who act like they know it all but sometimes yank out a vegetable instead of a weed.

The great thing about this system of pipes and hoses is that nothing gushes wastefully out of a huge drain pipe, threatening to drown a sleeping cat.

CeCe explains to her adult friend, "When we get the hose set, we can plant squash seeds on both sides of the berm, and water drips down into the soil to feed seedlings on both sides. We'll be conserving gallons and gallons of water. And we can grow two rows from the drip of one hose!"

Henry grins. "Two rows, one hose." He's a poet — and he gets it.

Chapter 20

CeCe Starts Sketching

CeCe leaves Otoña talking with the AGC folks. *I'm so mad at Mom. She's always in overdrive. She didn't say anything about the corn and squash, but I know she was blaming me. I guess I was stupid, but — I liked it better when dad was home, before that war. I wish…"*

I comprehend CeCe's desire to escape from her mom's constant stress. She grabs her satchel and skips along several interconnected pathways heading for the western part of the garden. Botanical Barb weeds the edge of her turf, observing a bird in the midst of their saffron patch. "Hi, CeCe," she whispers. "Come sit down and watch this mama bird. She's a shore bird — doesn't normally live here — but I think she's found the canal water. Just watch. Take out your sketch pad if you like."

A lady killdeer gathers strands of straw, string and other fuzz to build a nest on the ground in a row of saffron and Bok Choy. With only a slender beak as her tool, mama killdeer constructs a nest about six inches wide. Then she settles in to lay her eggs. CeCe studies the bird with reverence.

I, on the other hand, think, *if one day soon the local king snake doesn't gobble up the eggs, I might grab a baby bird for breakfast.* Just thinking ahead.

CeCe crouches down to observe the bird. She quietly slides her sketchbook and pencils out of the sack. She selects the black and brown pencils. She feels — more than hears — a voice whispering, "Watch it carefully. Notice every detail — the eyes, the beak, the two black marks on the chest." It's as if a muse guides her as she makes a draft, then a more accurate rendering of the nesting killdeer. She spends almost a half hour just watching and sketching.

Barb motions silently for her to come away and look at something else. A tarantula crosses the open path. Keeping her eye on the tarantula, she feels her sense of observation becoming keener, and the sketches improve.

Suddenly, she blurts out to Barb, "I'm such a failure, Barb! I insisted on planting the corn, beans and squash, and they all died. I'll never get gardening right."

Barb slides down on the ground and puts an arm around CeCe. "Oh, honey," she says, "we all have lessons to learn. Do you think I got it right the first time? I once planted tomatoes in the fall and a frost killed all of them that December. It takes practice and trying again. I'm sure your mom had her share of 'failed crops' when she first started gardening. But she and I have been gardening for years. I've even taken classes at the local botanical garden. Here's something that might help." She slips a flyer into CeCe's hand that lists all vegetables on one side and all flowers and herbs on the other, and all the best months in which they should be planted, for this 'planting zone' in Phoenix. "You know, there are about nine planting "zones" in the United States. They vary with the temperature, how hot it gets, how much it freezes, and the soil and humidity. People in Virginia do it differently from people in Massachusetts. It's way different even in Flagstaff. Having things not work out sometimes is part of the gardening process." She cradles CeCe into a comforting hug. They remain silent, CeCe feeling understood and Barb knowing she is needed.

After a few minutes, as CeCe studies the vegetable list, Barb mentions, "There are nine zones in the entire country, from coldest to warmest. We're warmest here. Everyone in every zone needs to know that crops can grow, and when to plant. You know, the Native Americans you thought of were mostly Hopi, Zuni and Navajo in northern Arizona and New Mexico. They had a different 'zone' and planting time, and I bet they too learned from trial and error."

After an hour, CeCe returns to Otoña's garden. "Mom, look at what Botanical Barb showed me. There's a planting time chart for all the vegetables. And it can be different in different climates." She pulls out her sketch pad. "There was a mama killdeer and a tarantula! I felt my muse, too, telling me how to draw. I'm going to find lots of animals in the garden."

The hairs on the back of Otoña's neck stiffen. "What do you mean, your muse talked to you?"

"I dunno. It's just, well, like, I feel guidance when I need it. I don't see or hear a real person. No, I'm sure it's not *Dad*." She emphasizes "Dad" to make sure Mom understands. "I just feel like someone — maybe Barb, or my instinct — is helping me become a better artist — or maybe an animal scientist."

Chapter 21

Saturday School #3
The Real Recidivists

March blows in. Big Joe calls another
Saturday School. He asks the Juvies —
Crabgrass and Clodbuster — to lead
the crowd in the stretch warm-up.
Zorro hangs out by Hurricane, who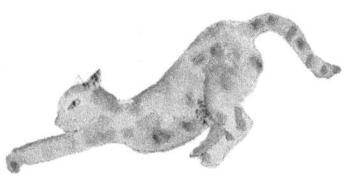
joins the group after setting up the amps and speakers. CeCe and
some girlfriends surround Darlene and Latifa.

Arms up to the sky, as if reaching for the heavens. Then a quick
fingers-to-toes, with a huge bend, and the "down cat" pose, with
feet on ground, hands on ground, sticking that old butt of yours, or
mine, toward the sun.

Big Joe launches into his morning sermon. "They say," he
says, pointing to the north side of the city, way beyond the garden,
"recidivism is a bad thing. They lock you up for doing something
they made illegal. And sometimes they just put a target on your back.
So they throw you inside."

By now, everyone who visits the garden knows that 'inside' is
the code word for 'prison.'

"So, having it brutally rough for years, you come back outside,
don't know how to live, can't find a place to live or get a job, get
caught at something, and 'strike three you're out'— and back inside.
They call that 'recidivism'. Like you keep doing the same dumb
stuff over and over. "Big Joe pauses for dramatic effect. He's a real
showman, Big Joe.

"But the real recidivists are here with us today. Aren't they?
Backhoe? Ike? Geronimo?" He walks around, gently clapping several
guys on the shoulder. Seems most of them tend toward the darker
shades of my brindle. Still, Zachariah is not anywhere close to the

circle. He stands at the far end of "Tarp Plaza," hidden from view behind a post. I saunter over and rub his socks.

"Yeah," says Ike. "Been out 15 years, still can't get a regular job. Started coming to the garden last May when it hadn't even begun." *Right, Ike, when you practically drowned me!* "Now I run the irrigation system for all the gardeners. I've learned a real job here with Big Joe."

"And I can bring my kids here, and they're safe, learn stuff and have fun," says Geronimo. This is my community. This is home." He gives Big Joe an *abrazo*. (That's Spanish for hug.)

Big Joe works the crowd. "So, my friends, the real recidivism is this. It's Ike, Geronimo, and you others (he names a few), — and me. We keep coming to the garden. We haul out weeds. We plant the seeds; we water the seedlings. We learn to make good compost. We learn every plant's water needs — none for the prickly pear, lots for the squash. We harvest the crops, wash and prepare them, and we sell our produce at farmer's markets. We learn to be counted on. It's like Latifa's Circle of Life, starting here, learning all the phases of what we do, and coming full circle to a harvest. Recidivism ain't a bad word. Here at the garden, it's good! You're looking at recidivism right here, right now."

Me? Of course I'm a recidivist. I was on my own for years before these crazies showed up, flooding my bedroom and causing the chaos that subsequently became a community garden.

"The main thing," Big Joe repeats, is that recidivism here at the garden is not bad — it's good! We're all recidivists of one kind or another — why not be community garden recidivists? — learning how to grow food, get along with each other, showing up every day, feeding our families and our community, and coming back for more."

Hurray! He's done. That guy can talk on and on.

The crowd applauds loudly. Big Joe's preaching to the choir, as they say. Then he divides them up into three groups — the weed pickers, the mulch managers, and the newcomers — the ones who aren't yet recidivists.

Chapter 22

Community Garden #102 Companion Plants

After the "recidivist" monologue, I notice several changes.

First, it is full-blown spring. April has arrived. The sun shines. Darlene has commandeered a team of recidivists and volunteers from churches and the local university to bring a few tractor-loads of compost to the chicken-coop area and they mix it in with the cardboard, duck poop — from a new duck — and fungi. They're grinding out healthy soil by the ton. They're tilling it into new sections of the garden that will be planted in the early fall, after it has "ripened."

Second, all sorts of plants are blooming and producing fruits and vegetables. Pomelos and pink grapefruit begin to grow on the citrus trees (to be ripe in December and next year). Tomatoes redden. Lettuce and kale abound.

Third, people are tending to all parts of the garden. They weed, hoe, and fight the pests that want to eat the vegetables they have grown for themselves, their families, and for needy folks in the community.

It's all part of the web of life. Animals are attracted to the plants for food — different plant, different animal. Bunnies like lettuce. gophers like chard and roots. Aphids like tomatoes. Lady bugs like aphids.

Some gardeners have planted garlic near chard as companion plants to deter the gophers. Basil, companion to tomatoes, will deter the moths that would like to lay hornworms. Basil also attracts bees who improve the pollination of tomatoes. A row of dill attracts ladybugs, which eat aphids, which are drawn to the tomatoes but then are eaten by the ladybugs. Yellow and orange nasturtiums lure carrot flies and caterpillars away from cabbage, broccoli and kale.

Some folks have planted sunflowers to support climbing cucumbers and pole beans, as well as to attract birds who eat the sunflower seeds.

Aside from companion plants, other deterrents reduce the potential carnage caused by veggie-pests. Netting and chicken wire prevent mockingbirds from nibbling seedlings. The Cooper's hawk zooms in to pick off field mice. The great horned owl scoops a scurrying vole in his talons. If Darlene were to chart it on her white board, it would look like a very tangled spider's web.

Speaking of which, numerous spiders weave their webs among the ochre plants and fling themselves on their silky strings from stalk to stalk.

Late one afternoon Zorro, CeCe and Otoña arrive after school. Theodora and a team of cooks from the retirement community have planned supper for everyone working here tonight. The sun sets later each day, giving gardeners more time after work or school to tend their crops.

CeCe has tried to draw the Cooper's hawk in flight, but found that the great horned owl, resting obscurely of the branches of a mulberry tree, was a better subject. This afternoon she fills a page with ladybugs eliminating the aphids that try to suck the leaves and stems of Darlene's Roma tomatoes.

I've noticed that Botanical Barb has sort of taken CeCe 'under her wing,' as people say. Barb has no wings, but she and CeCe are like companion plants. Barb teaches CeCe patience in her observations. CeCe fills a hole in Barb's childless life — like Zachariah fills a hole in mine.

Over by the mural (more on that soon), Zorro has latched on to Wiley and Hurricane. These two men have gifts to offer, and Zorro is 'lapping it up' (as the humans say — no cream involved). Latifa and Darlene befriend Otoña. Seems like just about everyone is a 'companion plant' to someone else. But when her girlfriends arrive, CeCe abandons Botanical Barb. Then Barb joins Latifa and Darlene and Otoña — the grown-up ladies.

Plants, animals, dirt, sun, water, people — and me. It's coming together, like a real community garden.

But, I wonder, *what about Sad Zach?*

Chapter 23

The Mural And The Road Map

Meanwhile, back at the mural, Wiley chats with a group of 'recidivists' who have been moving mulch, pruning trees, and installing drip-hoses in several of the family gardens.

These guys are of all ages. Some were 'inside' for a long time. You can see life has worn hard on them. The younger ones still don't seem 'broken' but they've learned — 'experience' is the word for it — that some risks are really bad for them, their loved ones, and any future of freedom. All of them are working on their own 'Personal Road Map'— a set of steps they've agreed to take — with a peer mentor — to put and keep their lives on track. They take it a day at a time.

As Zorro approaches the mural, Hurricane — the music man — heads for the plaza to put together a jazzy set to wrap up the end of the day.

Wiley has painted about twenty feet of the wall since last week. He's on the move!

"Hi, Zorro. Want to make art today? Here, put on this old shirt." Wiley grabs a large collared, buttoned long-sleeve shirt that once had seen fancy days but is now slathered in paint.

"Hi, Wiley. You bet."

Wiley gives Zorro a brush. "Follow me." He shows Zorro how to paint an orange background, drifting into yellow.

People come over and schmooze. The paint dries, and Wiley adds green tasseled corn stalks against the yellow-orange background. Then he moves to the right, heading south, to paint a beige pot with black indigenous designs. Pouring from the pot gushes a huge stream of blue water that resembles waves in an ocean — what it looked like that early morning last May when water flooded through the pipe and threw me up against a berm! They talk about the colors. I can't tell the difference, but I can sense the movement of water gushing from the pot. The memory makes me shiver.

Ignoring my feelings, the visitors launch into a long discussion about how vital water is to our garden. Without water, we can't grow any crops — no tomatoes, pepitas, corn, or cabbage! They praise Wiley for his beautiful water art. They comment on Ike's great job improving the irrigation.

Next, Wiley paints a woman with skin the color of pecans and smooth as clay, with mahogany hair and eyes, like the rich loamy earth after good compost has biodegraded and made the soil nutritious again. "Look closely at what you're about to paint," Wiley guides Zorro. "The more carefully you observe, the more accurate your paintbrush will be."

Soon, Wiley and Zorro paint rows and rows of vegetables — little seedlings, then bigger plants a few weeks older, and finally rows of full-grown lettuces and carrots, tomatoes and peppers, all ready to be harvested. Doesn't appeal to me, but the humans applaud.

Soon Tiger appears in the mural wearing a pyramid-circle shaped basket-hat to fend off the hot sun. Tiger breaks into a smile. "I've never been painted before!" He returns to his crew of volunteers to harvest crops for the local Farmers' Market. He's pleased as punch with his portrait.

Zorro adds sand and mountains with a bunch of saguaro cacti, majestic against a painted blue sky. Wiley inserts a group of the children playing tag, then a moringa tree with its low-hanging bean-filled pods. He includes something of almost everyone and everything in the garden by the time he makes his way to the south end of the wall, where it stops at the sidewalk.

After cleaning his brushes, Zorro hits the trail straight over to Hurricane.

Wiley is just about to wrap it up when I creep out from under the Palo Verde tree shading the Little Library. I introduced myself.

"Meow," I say, *I am Sebastian, the local feral cat. Pretty nice job you've done painting the garden.* "Meeeeoooowwww."

"Well, I'll be!" exclaims Wiley. "I hadn't noticed you before."

Of course not. I've been spying on you.

"Let me get a good look at you, cat," he says. "May I paint you into our mural?" He wipes off a brush and grabs a few tubes of acrylic — brown and black and grey and tan and white — brindle, like me.

Did I say I was the handsomest cat in this entire community garden? I don't want to boast, but I think it would be ever so fitting for the artist to include a portrait of this fine-looking feline. I sit down, stick up one of my hind legs, and start licking myself to get clean. I'm just about ready to pose for him when he says, "Done! Finished! Nice job, cat. As far as portraits go, you are the cat's meow. Get it? Ha, ha." He apparently thinks he's funny.

I look at his handiwork. If I were anyone but a feral tomcat, I might be embarrassed. But he did paint a good likeness. "Meeooww," I agree.

Chapter 24

Solving One Mystery

Theodora's team rings a loud gong. Dinner's ready. Hurricane has set up the mixers, amps and laptop, and hip-hop blasts forth from the speakers. CeCe and some girlfriends get in line and fill their plates with chicken drumsticks, mashed potatoes, and salad. They cluster at one table. The moms sit at another. Between the music and the chit-chat, everyone seems to be having a good time.

Meanwhile, where's Zorro? He has left the mural, checks in only for a quick minute with Hurricane, and then he heads north. He maneuvers between the prickly pear clusters. He's headed for the Healing and Pollinator Garden.

That's my home turf, and Sad Zach's, too. I trot over. Zorro still wears Wiley's shirt. Dabs of paint on his face and hands signal the emergence of a young artist.

I land on a crest of a small rise on the southern edge of the Healing Garden. Someone has planted catnip — a plus for me.

Stopping abruptly — near me — Zorro picks mindlessly at some mesquite pods, popping the seeds into a zip-lock bag in his satchel. His gaze moves across the sunken center of the area, to the hillock on the north side of the gully, where Sad Zach rests on his haunches, twisting some grass into a long skinny braid.

Zach keeps his gaze fixed on Zorro. Zorro stands absolutely still, his big paint shirt flapping gently in the breeze. He stares silently back.

OMG, they look alike. For all I can tell, they come from the same litter! Except Zach is old and Zorro is young.

After a long silence, Zorro whispers, "Dad?" In the stillness of the Healing Garden, his voice travels tentatively, like a strand of spider silk, across the depression in the sand to the northern rise.

Sad Zach whispers back, "Zorro. Son."

They don't move.

I creep closer. I feel a monumental shift happening — not underground, or through the irrigation pipe that almost cost my life, but across the airwaves of this dry, quiet northeast nook, the most protected space in the whole garden.

"I thought you were in prison, Dad. I heard maybe you got out. I thought — You've been here all along, haven't you?"

He starts to choke up. I have to help him out. I rub my brindle back against his dirty legs. Startled, he looks down at me. Then he realizes I'm trying to tell him, *It's OK, Zorro. I'm your friend. Don't worry.*

"I was." Sad Zach brushes a hand across his eyes. I see a wet dirty smudge on his cheeks. "I got out a year ago. I was homeless for a while. I actually slept here in the garden, on that crummy couch over there," — he points vaguely. "But when the garden started last May, Big Joe found me. He's been helping me get back on my feet. I'm in a half-way house, and —" he stops. "I'm not supposed to see you and CeCe or talk to you at all. I screwed it up so bad with your mom!" He turns his head away, pounding the dirt, as if to punish himself.

This ain't right. He obviously loves his kid. I dash across the sandy patch, the lemony scent from a rosemary bush fragrant in the early evening air.

"Meow!" I call to Sad Zach. "Meow!" *Hold on a minute! I'm your friend, too, remember? Here I am.* "Purr." I whip my tail around his ankle.

Zorro looks at me, then at Zach. "You know that cat? He's *our* friend, CeCe's and mine. Looks like he knows you too. What —?"

Sad Zach plunks himself on the dirt where he had crouched. He catches my tail and softly, slowly, strokes it all the way to its tip. He reaches into the grubby sack next to him and pulls out a can of tuna and dumps some straight onto the ground. "Here, Sebastian," he says, "Sorry I've missed so many days. This can is albacore."

Like I care whether it's albacore. It's tuna! Sad Zach has thought of *me* again. "Purr!" *Schlurrrp.*

Zorro had started to walk away. But he suddenly turns back and says, "Hey! You know the cat's name?"

"Well, he kept me company the many nights I slept here, before Big Joe found me a place to stay." Sad Zach gently strokes my tail again. "He's been my best friend. He's one right classy cat, don't you think? So I gave him a classy name — Sebastian."

"Sebastian. I like that. Hi, Sebastian." Zorro waves to me from across the ditch.

The two look-alikes pause, drawn to each other but forbidden to savor the moment.

"I won't tell Mom," Zorro says. "I'll just say I was looking for Sebas — I mean, the cat."

Sad Zach shakes his head. "No, kiddo, it's not right to lie to your mom. You gotta tell her the truth. You found me. But I didn't hit nobody or nothing. 'I'm working on my PTSD and what the pros call 'anger management'."

Hit somebody? Of course not. But then again, Sad Zach is here, and Zorro is there. Besides, he has been nothing but gentle and generous with me. So, it's absurd.

Zorro cries, "But she'll be furious! She'll never let me come to the garden again. I won't be allowed to see you — or Sebastian." He studies his Jordan Air knock-offs and toes the ground.

"Well, you still gotta tell her. It's the right thing to do."

Zorro hesitates. "Are you sure? I remember how mad she was. And you went crazy! But you aren't really like that"...

Sad Zach insists. "Yep. But ask her to talk to Big Joe. He might"— He pauses, seems to think about his next phrase. "And you can tell CeCe the cat's name is Sebastian." He puts forth a wobbly attempt at a smile.

At that point a ruckus can be heard under the tarps. Hurricane has set up the mixer, his laptop, the amps and speakers. He's upped the volume and the kids are dancing. "Gotta go," says Zorro," and he scoots through a bower of pomegranate bushes.

However, Zorro doesn't go straight to the music. He finds his sister, takes her hand and pulls her behind a six-foot-high row of sugar cane.

"What's up Z?" I was just about to"— CeCe tries to loosen his grip.

"CeeC, calm down. Listen to me." Zorro drops his voice to a whisper. "Way over there in the Healing Garden, I just saw Dad! We talked. And I have to tell Mom. He told me to tell the truth. But I thought you should know first."

"How are we gonna handle this? Mom has that Order of Protection. She doesn't want us ever to see him again." CeCe looks deep into Zorro's eyes. "How is he? Is he OK? He went crazy that day he hurt Mom. But he's not really like that." She peers through all the trees and bushes, as if she can catch a glimpse of her dad. "I want to see him again. He's been here the whole time, hasn't he?"

Now I get it. How Zach would watch the kids from a distance but never go near. How art supplies arrived in Toña's garden that were exactly what each kid needed.

Chapter 25

Bats And Gnats

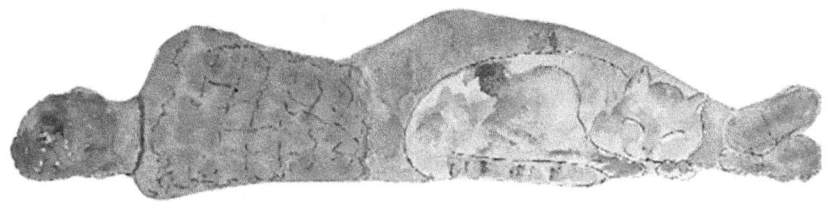

It's a warm dark May evening. The sun has set. Sad Zach shows up, by surprise, and seeks out his abandoned couch. He digs a tin can out of one bag — for me. In the other hand he's carrying a big red Dr. Dan. He dishes out some tuna. I'm ready to gobble it down.

The tuna comes with a price — Zach wants to talk.

"Hey, Sebastian, I've got the evening off from the half-way house for good behavior. Tuna for you, Dr. Dan for me. Big Joe said I could come out to the Healing Garden. You may not have noticed this, — "but the plants are healthier these days."

Why should I care? As long as there are mice and baby birds around, and when Sad Zach shows up with his can of tuna, life is good. But he seems to think I — a carnivore to the core — should know about plant health.

"So, Sebastian, I've been learning about the 'Circle of Life'."

Sounds to me a lot like Latifa's 'circle of life,' and I consider taking a nap. But that can of tuna keeps me awake and occupied, so I oblige him by listening. "Everything has its place, friend cat. It starts with the plants, and the insects, and the worms and moths and such. Bugs can do a huge amount of damage to plants."

He takes a long sip through a straw of his Dr. Dan.

"By the way, Sebastian, do you notice how I've switched my evening beverage to something that doesn't need a paper bag?"

He pauses. I have noticed. Fortunately he has not changed the routine of bringing tuna fish as well. I am pleased about that. I don't know what the Dr. Dan means, but he seems proud of himself. So I stop stuffing my face and give him a "meow." A nice "meow," then a "purr," to let him know I'm paying attention and I approve of whatever he is doing — especially the fish.

He gets back to the 'Circle of Life'. "So, Sebastian, I'll tell you what I'm learning in this book from the library," he says, taking the book from under his arm and opening it. "The plants grow, and the insects want to eat them. But in fly the bats, who swarm out here by the thousands — at night — to eat moths and other insects, including gnats, that might try to prey on the plants."

Good enough, can you please dish out a little more tuna?

"So you need to know about how wonderful bats are, Sebastian. There's a colony of them in a man-made-above-ground tunnel-cave just a few miles from here. The bats are Mexican Free-Tailed Bats — so named because they winter in Mexico and because their tails extend out beyond their bottoms, which in many bats they do not."

I cannot imagine a tail *not* extending beyond my bottom. My tail swishes slowly when I'm stalking and wraps gently around ankles to say *You're OK.* And with the right human, my tail loves being stroked.

He sucks too fast on his straw and practically inhales some liquid. He snorts it out his nose and grabs a napkin to clean up the snot and spray.

"So here's what's amazing — *amazing!* — about bats," he says. They can fly at night. They don't really see very well at night. I don't either. How about you?"

I say "meow." I don't see color, like you humans, I see more grays and stuff, but I can track a moving mouse or vole at dusk and catch it in a heartbeat. That is part of my great circle of life — the mice eat the breadcrumbs and insects, and I eat the mice.

"So," he continues, "bats navigate at night by echolocation. Get it, Sebastian? They can locate something by sending out a message — which, by the way, is at a pitch too high for humans to hear — and those bats can hear the echo bouncing off the object — like a moth, or a gnat! Echo-location. Isn't that amazing?"

I'm having a hard time getting this, but I pretend. "Meow."

"It's not like how you and I hear," I hear him say with my very sharp cat ears. "When we listen and hear stuff," he says, "we just passively receive noise made by someone or something else. But bats emit or send out little sounds that bounce back off things. And, by the way the sound bounces back, or echoes, and by the way the bats hear that little sound, they can tell if it's a building they don't want to bump into or a gnat that's flying nearby. Then they can fly over and gobble up that gnat in the tiny teeth of their tiny little bat mouth."

I keep nibbling tuna. I could use a drink just now. I look at him. He pours some Dr. Dan into my tuna can. It looks like water. I take a sip.

Yuk! What's in that? I spit it out and continue on with the tuna.

"I'm sorry," he says, "I thought you might like something to drink."

I would, but not that. Anyway, I digress.

"So," he says, wrapping up his lesson to this cat on the bats, "there's a 'Circle of Life'. The insects eat the crumbs, and the bats eat the insects, and the bats poop guano, which — as Darlene tells everyone — is very nutritious. When it falls onto the ground and gets mixed into the dirt, the seeds that we humans plant will grow into healthier plants."

Sad Zach shuts his mouth, taking a break. It was a long lesson. And he has missed one very valuable fact — if I could catch a bat, I would eat it. The 'Circle of Life' would be bigger and rounder — and better, with me included.

But the bats, especially the Mexican Free-Tailed bats that fly from the man-made tunnel a few miles away and spread out by the hundreds over our many little gardens — these flying bats stay up in the air and make it impossible for me to complete the circle. Life can be hard for a feral cat.

After drinking all that Dr. Dan, Sad Zach suddenly stands up to visit the bushes to — as he says — 'see a man about a horse'. Just as suddenly, from out of the evening sky, a bat bumps into him and falls onto the couch. It's echo-location has failed because Zach moved too quickly. Zach wasn't there when the bat emitted its little screech, and the screech didn't bounce off him. But there he was there a split second later when he stood up. Bam and whammo! Bat zooms into Zach and does a bounce on the couch.

Sad Zach jumps away from it as if it has rabies! It probably doesn't, but bats can bite people when handled, so handling bats is a no-no.

Now is my chance! Did I tell you that bats are — whenever possible — part of *my* circle of life? They are delicious small mammals. I look on that little bat-who-was-not-paying-attention as a possible dinner! I leap up onto the couch, but this guy has come to his senses and flies away, paying more attention to his echo-location. Did I get that right? Occasionally bats don't pay attention, or they read their signals wrong (who is perfect, besides me?) and they can bump into things, or people. Still, this bat reacts fast. I lose out.

Sad Zach has recovered his senses and returned from the bushes. He sits down on the couch, motioning for me to jump back up and take a snooze with him. "I gotta tell you one more thing I learned in this book," he says. "There is a tropical bat called a vampire bat. It feeds mostly on cows. It walks on the ground up to its prey — the cow —, takes a bite of the animal, and drinks its blood. There's something called 'draculin' in the bat's saliva that keeps the blood from coagulating, so the bat can sit there and drink blood (from the cow, not a human) for up to an hour. Pretty ghoulish, don't cha think? I bet that's where Count Dracula the Vampire got his name — from the substance in the vampire bat's blood."

I do find that whole thing pretty ghoulish. More to the point, Zach's voice has smoothed out and slowed down. He doesn't seem so sad. I'm glad he's back, even if for just one night. Now, curled up against his backside, I sleep.

Chapter 26

Community Garden #103
A Couple of Quiet Pow-Wows

The next day in the late afternoon I find Big Joe and a whole crew of recidivist workers who have shoveled mulch, yanked weeds, and pruned up the low tree branches all day. For several months now, Sad Zach has been developing leadership skills as part of the crew. He's as hot and sweaty as the rest of them, and they've all headed over to the solar-paneled hot waterspouts to get a bucket or two to pour over themselves and clean up.

Big Joe is about to leave when I see Otoña come into the garden and head for her individual plot. Zorro has found a bunch of schoolmates. They are off in the western section of garden that hosts a family of Gambel's quail and an occasional coyote. The boys seem bent on catching something.

CeCe, meanwhile, heads for the chicken coop. She'll draw ducks and chickens.

The main thing I notice is that this whole human family's body language says that no one wants to talk to each other. I wonder what's up.

I see Zach soaked to the bone from hosing off after the day's work. Pretty funny looking, except that I can tell he's tense.

Joe heads over toward Otoña's plot where she is vigorously digging weeds out from around the young orange tree they planted last fall. She seems bound and determined not to notice anyone.

Joe comes over, facing her, so close that if she stands up she'll bump into him.

"Otoña," he says in his deep strong voice. It's a statement, not a question.

She keeps on digging.

"It's me, Big Joe, 'Toña."

"I know. Now go away."

"I'm not leaving until we've talked."

"I don't wanna." Loud, like she means it. Then, "I don't wanna," soft, on the verge of something else.

"You know Zachariah is here, don't you?" he says to her.

She nods.

"Do you also know that he and Zorro met at the Healing Garden?"

Another nod. A turning of her head toward where she knows Zachariah stands, soaked, then to CeCe at the chicken coop, finally out to Zorro at the northwestern edge. Then Otoña suddenly slumps to the ground sobbing.

I consider trotting over to her, rubbing up against her side. But she and I don't know each other that well. I keep my distance.

Joe crouches down close to her. "He's changed, 'Toña. I know it was real bad after he came back from Afghanistan. That war damaged him. I know he was unpredictable, violent. It was *not* OK. I know that as much as you."

"How can you?" She almost spits the words at Big Joe. "You weren't there when"...

"I was like that too," he says. "Not from the war, but from my neighborhood. I wound up in a gang, and we all did bad stuff, even to those we loved. I'm not proud of who I was."

"He broke my ribs! That's when we called the cops. I wound up in the hospital! He needed to go to prison. A crazy, violent man! He was trying to kill me!"

"I know it was awful. But we also didn't know about PTSD from the war, how it can attack a vet, sneak into his nightmares, make him a madman. That's what was happening to Zachariah, and we didn't know."

"So I'm supposed to forget all that?"

Joe pauses, breathes in deep, and lets out a long slow sigh. "No, 'Toña, no. I'm just asking you to consider a few things. I don't think, when he was his real self, he would ever hurt you. But after the war, with the PTSD, he had unpredictable rages. Now he's also done two years inside. He was basically tossed back out without any money or a plan. Even though he was homeless and on the street, he found AA and is trying to get sober." *I finally understand the shift from the bottle in the bag to the Dr. Dan. Zach has been trying to clean up his act.*

"He's staying in a halfway house. The VA has helped him get counseling for his PTSD. He also meets weekly with a Vets' peer group. I had PTSD too, from the gang fights and from my time inside."

She looks startled. "You did time?"

"Oh, yeah. More than once. It's not that I'm not ashamed of what I did to get there — I am. But it's what prison does to a man. It's brutal. If you didn't have PTSD before, you might get it there. Your Zach has been through a lot, and he's trying hard to turn his life around."

"He's not 'my Zach'," she says. Then she turns to Big Joe and just sobs into his shoulder. "Oh, Joe, I loved him so much!"

Big Joe just holds her and stays silent. Something I didn't know he could do. After a few minutes, he picks up where he left off.

"So Toña, here's what I see. I see a man who now does AA, does PTSD counseling, and who has complied with the rules of a halfway house. He comes to the garden four, five, six days a week. He hauls trash, digs compost, and takes direction from Tiger, Ike, Latifa and Darlene about how to grow healthy food for our neighborhood. He keeps coming. He's even coaching the Juvies. And — you know he's here today."

She nods.

"I believe the kiddos — Zorro and Cecilia — want to see him, but they don't want to hurt you. They witnessed and experienced more than we adults realize. They hurt more than we ever want them to. But they are resilient, they can heal. Toña, I believe they both want to spend time with their dad."

"Meow." I know Big Joe is on the right track.

"Hey, cat," he says. Then, "Hey, Sebastian, Zachariah tells me that's your name. It's a good name. I hope you like it. What do you think of all this?"

I don't know how he knows that I know, but I know what's going on and he knows I know. I do one of those "purrs" that vibrates out of my throat and can be felt more than heard. Taking a big risk, for the first time I "purr" up against Big Joe's jeans.

Well, Big Joe seems to catch on that everyone's skittish. We've all been dealt some bad stuff. He doesn't touch me — that's smart, because he doesn't know me that well — but he gives me that slow eye-blink thing that says, lashes and lids down — "I," — lashes and lids slowly back up, eyes open, "like you." I gaze straight back at him. *I'm with you, I'm in on this conversation.*

Meanwhile, Otoña studies the both of us. She realizes that something new is happening. "So, what can I do, Joe? I'm so scared."

"No need to rush things, 'Toña," says Big Joe. "Here's where I'd start. How about I walk with Zorro and CeCe — if they'll tear themselves away from the chickens and quail — out to the Healing Garden, where Zorro first encountered Zachariah."

I notice Big Joe does not call him 'Sad Zach'.

"And" he continues, "I think if Zach sees me walking over there, he'll follow me from the clean-up corner. However, I can let him know with just a nod that he has to stand at some distance. Do you want to come too?"

"I don't know," she mumbles. Then, "What if?"

"If he gets out of hand? Don't worry, I'll be there. I can flatten him in a heartbeat, and he knows it."

"But what if the kids want to"…

"Hug him? You're right, they will want to hug him. He'll be afraid — mostly of himself — but he'll want to hug them too. Trust me, 'Toña, I'll be there. I think they can hug, and nobody will get hurt."

"What about after that?"

"One step at a time. I'll ask him to have his counselor and his parole officer contact you. The garden is a great place to meet.

It's safe, and there is so much stuff to do. If we can get one of his supervisors to be present, we could set up meetings."

"I can't take him back!" She throws up a last defense.

"No one ever said you have to. Let's not get ahead of things. Listen, My wife still keeps me at arm's length when I"...

'Toña seems to have found a safe point. "OK, if you'll be with them."

The next thing I know, Big Joe has sent out a piercing whistle and Zorro and CeCe come running at a fast clip, through brambles, up and down ridges, jumping over plants and rocks and ducking under trees.

Zachariah heard the whistle too. Seems like everyone but 'Toña and me knew in advance about the signal. Zach wrestles off his sweaty shirt, dons a clean one, and walks the long way around over by the mural toward the Healing Garden — where he first encountered Zorro.

I trot under cover of low-hanging citrus trees and pounce over to Zachariah. I think he needs a sidekick. "Meow," *I'm here if you need me.*

Joe, Otoña and the kiddos arrive at the space near the prickly pear cactus where Zorro stood before. Joe waves. "Hi, Zachariah. I"ve been chatting with Otoña here, and she says it's OK if you and CeCe and Zorro all get re-acquainted. You down with that?"

"Yeah." I can hardly hear Sad Zach, even sitting right next to him. He's sort of choked up. "Yeah."

"So the kids and I are gonna cross though this DMZ — this de-militarized zone — of desert lavender to come say 'hi.' OK?"

"OK." You can tell Sad Zach is as nervous as it gets without wetting his pants. He hasn't been near his kids, from war and prison, for the most of five years.

Zorro and CeCe start to run. "Not so fast," says Big Joe. I'm the boss of this here reunion, and you kids have to go at my pace." He walks with extra deliberate care, as if the prickly pear is going to turn into jumping cholla and attack him personally. Zorro and CeCe stop and match his pace.

Finally they cross that very small, scented valley of healing plants — the lavender, the rosemary, and the moringa tree with its enormous pods. They reach Zachariah's little rise. "Dad," they both say, and they hug him.

Daddy Zach hugs back. From where I crouch, six legs bump into each other and six arms wrap into a love-circle around the three bodies. Across the way, Otoña looks on, nervous. I wonder how she feels. I stay put. This is Zachariah's moment.

Finally Big Joe breaks up the love fest. "Knock it off, guys," he cajoles the reluctant trio. "Zachariah, I'm glad we figured out a way for the kiddos to be able to greet you in this Garden of Healing. But I gotta get back to the crowd. Otoña has to finish watering her plants. Zorro and CeCe have friends their own age to hang out with."

Zach disassembles the mass of smaller body parts from his own. "Thanks, Big Joe." And "Hello, 'Toña," he calls timidly across the lavender sea.

Then, for all to hear real clearly, he says, "Thank you, Big Joe. Thank you Toña. I am so sorry. So very sorry." He looks like he might cry but he doesn't. He shakes Big Joe's hand. "Anything you guys tell me, I'll do. I am so grateful for this moment."

And then I watch as the kids depart with Big Joe and their mom, leaving Daddy Zach on his haunches, recovering on his mound of sand in the Healing Garden.

Chapter 27

Smoothie Saturday

It's really early on this May Saturday, but Zorro comes running down a path and over to where he found me last time. It is the twins' birthday today. It's almost a year since the garden officially began. They are finally thirteen — teenagers!

"Hey, Sebastian!" Zorro calls softly. "Come on out. We're gonna do smoothies today. Come see!"

I'm independent, so I don't follow him right away. I've got my pride. Soon I slink over to the pavilion where CeCe has joined a few girlfriends and Zorro is hanging out with the boys who do not — quite — acknowledge the existence of the girls.

It's hot today. It's mid-May and we've had no rain for over a month — just lots of sun. Big Joe is kinda sweaty after they do the stretches. He asks all the young people to come around this table in the shade. Some of the adults have placed fruit, yogurt, nuts and other veggies on the table. Off to the side there's an extension cord to provide electricity, which the garden doesn't otherwise possess.

This is a good thing — if there were electricity, all sorts of people would come in at night and bring their TVs. They would light up the night sky and confuse the dickens out of the nocturnal birds, bats and insects. These fellow creatures rely on darkness when they enter the garden seeking plants — or fellow creatures to nibble on.

The old ladies from the retirement home have used one of the outside outlets on their building across the street to lay a 200-foot extension cord right on the road, over the dirt, and up to the table. Its purpose is to power the blender. Otoña and some other moms have brought different foods, some from the garden, to show how you can make healthy food that tastes delicious.

"Which do you want, chard or kale?" she asks the kids.

"Kale? Yuck!" snorts Zorro. "Ain't gonna get *me* to eat kale!" Some of the boys snicker in agreement.

"Not chard," whines CeCe in a snarky retort.

I'm surprised. They've been pretty keen on our garden so far.

'Toña rebounds with a "Wait 'till you taste this!" And corrals Zorro and four of his friends. "I dare you to not like it." She rings the boys around the table and plugs in — but does not turn on — the blender. "First, let's all wash our hands in this bowl of water."

All the kids seem willing to get a little wet. After all, it's a warm day. They use paper towels to dry off, which 'Tonya throws into a compost bucket. The paper will biodegrade, along with the left-over food scraps, plus some 'fun-gi,' into good soil for the next round of crops.

"We'll let the boys make this one," she dictates. After all, Zorro is fifteen minutes older than his sister. "There'll be enough for everyone to have a taste. If you like it, the girls will make the next one."

"Kyree," she says, "c'mon, chop this banana." He chops the banana. "Now put it in the blender." He scoops up the pieces and gently dumps them in.

"Next, Band-aid, cut this apple up and put it in the blender." Band-aid slices carefully. He successfully avoids adding any blood from a careless cut. "Good job," she comments. He lifts the slices into the blender.

"Now, 'Duardo, can you measure 1/2 cup of these strawberries that Mr. Meyerson grew in his berry patch?"

"'Duardo lights up. He's already sampled some of those garden-grown strawberries. They're smaller but sweeter than store-bought. He grabs a fistful of the chopped red bits and stuffs them into the measuring cup. He brings the cup up to eye level to be sure he got a little more than one-half.

"Zorro, how 'bout you pour in the special spoonful of 'preferred protein powder'?" Zorro complies. Protein is good for you and doesn't taste bad if it's in a cup of milk or yogurt and berries. Plus, Mom's the boss. Everyone else has obeyed, so he had better cooperate too.

"Alejandro, can you pour in a cup of soy milk?" Done.

Finally, Otoña takes a handful of chopped kale and pours it on top of all the rest. The kids groan.

"Wait 'till you've tried it," she coaches, "wait and see. But first, each one of you, place an ice cube in the blender. Five sets of chilly fingers gingerly drop in an ice cube.

"Now — and this is important," she pauses for emphasis, "each one of you put one hand on top of the blender, or on top of your friend's hand which is already on top of the blender. When I turn it on, it's gonna whir and shake. If you don't press tight, the top will blow off and we'll have 'kale gunk' all over your arms and faces and in your mouths before you can say 'strawberry smoothie.'"

I'm intrigued. Somehow Otoña has come out of her workaholic shell and acts as the mob boss. The boys all obey when she gives the orders. I look at how the guys put their hands on the black blender top, one by one. Another array of earth-tones, beautifully brindle, like me.

Otoña pushes the "ON" button. Wow! This blender shakes and rocks like it's got ants in its pants. The boys, shocked at first, press down with surprised determination. After three seconds she turns it off. "Take a deep breath, then on it goes again," she warns. More buzzing, rattling and whirring, but those tan, sandy and mahogany hands hold the blender top firmly in place.

Another three seconds and it's done. "Who's game for a sip of "strawberry banana kale smoothie," asks Otoña, with a wicked smile.

Well, they'd all been a part of making the thing, so 'Duardo steps up right away. "I'll try some." 'Toña pours. The other boys all grab paper cups and get their share. There's enough left for the girls to have some too.

"Hey," cheers Band-Aid, "this is great!"

"Told ya so," grins Zorro. "I knew it all along." CeCe sniggers. "What a fib that is!" But she likes it too. Doesn't even taste any kale — the banana and strawberry flavors win the day.

Otoña leads the girls in the next round. First, she cleans the blender under the water tap in the industrial-sized sink that has been hooked up nearby. More willingly, now that everyone has tasted success, the girls share the job of putting in a cup of chopped chard, one chopped banana, 3/4 cup of vanilla yogurt, a cup of raspberries, two tablespoons of pecans, and one-half cup of coconut water, a tablespoon of protein powder, plus one cube of ice from each girl.

The whirring, blending, shaking, and tasting all repeat.

"Meow?" I want to know what all the accolades were about. CeCe takes the top from the blender, turns it upside down, puts it on the ground, and pours in some smoothie. I gingerly step forward and take a lap,… lap, lap! *That's delicious!* To me, the yogurt wins out. The pecans, chard and raspberries play second fiddle to the milky vanilla. I lick all the edges, in and out — just doing my part, ya know, to clean the top as best I can.

Big Joe wanders over. "Where's *my* smoothie?" he pouts. Latifa also suddenly seems to need a health drink. With a chuckle, Otoña whips up a third batch — strawberry mango spinach smoothie. The three of them polish off the whole mix.

Saturday smoothies win the day.

Chapter 28

Marley

It's the third Saturday in May. School's out and things are bound to quiet down for the summer. But it's also almost one year since the community garden began. It's come a long way! Next Saturday they'll have the award ceremony for whoever did the most to create this community garden.

The 'recidivists' have taken truckloads of fresh produce to the farmers' markets on Wednesdays and Saturdays. Barb and Darlene are in charge of the official table of produce at our pavilion. Neighbors and visitors come and pay what they can afford to add nutritious greens, tomatoes, eggplant, and squash to their diet.

CeCe, part of the sales team, charms people into buying bunches of radishes and kale. Wiley has finished the mural, so Zorro has set his sights on Hurricane and the music set-up. Country and jazz instrumentals provide a backdrop for the morning goings-on. Over at the community tub, Otoña washes beets and carrots.

Big Joe leaves his crew of volunteers and recidivists and ambles over to where she is drying her cleaned veggies and rubber-banding them into buy-sized clumps. I notice how he stands quietly — uncharacteristically, for him — and waits until she seems ready to talk. I see their heads bend forward. I can't hear any of the words. Body language tells me there's no argument between them.

I decide to seek more action and head over to the incubator garden. The coulda-been-juvenile-delinquent guys are delicately digging baby cukes, beans and scallions from their tiny containers, carrying them ever-so-carefully, and plopping them gently into waiting holes in the berm. This section is newly equipped with the rubber drip hose that will save gallons of water but give plenty to the little seedlings.

At the center of the group — providing them with calm, expert guidance — is Zachariah. He's been a recidivist in the garden for almost a year now, since the time he switched to soda. Big Joe has put him on staff part-time. A large grant (whatever that is) seems to provide for this arrangement — like the manna from heaven I mentioned early on — an unexpected but totally wonderful gift.

But what's this? There's a dog — you heard me, a dog — by Zachariah's side, sitting quietly but alert, on a leash, wearing some kind of a vest.

Zach is my friend, not yours, I hiss, as I bound over and glare at him. But Zach spots me right away and says, "Hi, Sebastian. I want you to meet my new dog friend, Marley. He's a trained service dog, and he helps me with my PTSD."

How in heaven can a dog help my pal Zach? But Marley just sits there calmly, looks at me, and gives me the "I'm OK, you're OK" look. It's two species to one. I sit down.

You humans probably don't know this, but we other species can communicate, even without talking, meowing or barking. He looks at me calmly and says, through his look, "I know you. You're Zach's friend. I have no argument with you — unless you attack him. I'm here to warn him of any danger, and you're not a danger. So, Sebastian, let's just chill. I'll be Zachariah's service dog, protect him from danger, and you'll be his other best friend."

I don't like the "other" part of "best friend," but it's clear that he has no problem with me, and that Zach is friends to both of us. I remain on my haunches and monitor the scene.

Chapter 29

The Bomb

Zach talks quietly, giving hints and intervening when necessary, but letting these young bucks try things on their own. They mostly do it right. And they're feeling pretty good about this transplant, because Mentor Zach was with them a month ago when they  planted the seeds. They — and he — have showed up almost every day to be sure they got enough water in their compost-enriched soil, out in that glorious sun. They've seen the little first leaves pop out of the soil and then grow the next pair, droop a little if they didn't get enough to drink, and then stand up straight when our young petty criminals came back and turned on the irrigation.

I'm not kidding about the 'petty criminal' charge. Some of these kids are on probation from Juvenile Court and have to do community service time. Several live in group homes. A few of them came with a big attitude. All of them broke one law or another. Yet, after duty with either Ike — on how to run the irrigation system — or Darlene — on how to make compost — or Backhoe, Tiger and Geronimo — on how to haul mulch and nurture the plants — these guys start to get along. They learn that Big Joe and Zachariah did time and are here to say it's not worth it.

They've watched Backhoe provide knowledge and Geronimo give recidivism a good name. They began grudgingly. One or two have faltered along the way. Some picked fights with each other and Big Joe had to suspend them. A few dropped out for awhile. Most of them come back. They've learned that there are rules to follow, and screwing up has consequences — but there are second, sometimes even third chances. They also realize that the chances come from guys who know what it was like *not* to get a second chance.

Suddenly Big Joe corners Zachariah. "Hey."

"Hey." Daddy Zach leans on a rake. Joe and Zach exchange introductions with Marley. Of course, they both know me already.

Joe starts. "If I give you a $20, do you think you can pick out some veggies for the guys at the halfway house for dinner tonight? They sure can use a hand. Geronimo has a stir-fry recipe that even you can cook."

"What's the catch?" Zach spots a hook.

"No catch," answers Big Joe. "It's money the halfway house gave me to spend. You might as well be the guy who does the food shop."

"You know that's not what I meant," Zach parries. "There's a gimmick, somewhere. Be straight with me. I got my big boy pants on. I can handle a curve."

"Can't pull nothin' over on you," smiles Big Joe. "So, the deal is this. You and I saunter over to the garden grocery table. Darlene and Latifa keep track of the money. Meanwhile, there's also an attractive mom with her daughter. The daughter is an ace at selling you any used car on the lot. Watch out you don't just buy kale."

"And who might this lady and her daughter be?"

"That's for you to recognize, and to take in stride." Big Joe places a hand gently but firmly on Zachariah's arm and dislodges the rake. He looks admiringly down at Marley, who just looks at him calmly. It seems that Big Joe gets the deal with Marley too. "You ready?"

"But there's an Order of Protection out against me! I really appreciate that meeting in the Healing Garden. But that was a one-off. I can't"…

"In this particular instance," answers Joe, "with a table heaped with fresh vegetables between you and the young lady and her mom, it appears that someone has granted a temporary, conditional exception. Besides, I can take you down in less time than it takes to say"…

"Don't remind me!" Zach grins. "I'll give it my best effort. Lead the way, oh Great Master."

We leave the Juvies tending their tomato babies and I quietly follow Big Joe, Daddy Zach, and Marley, who trots cooperatively near Zach. They take the weedless wood chip path from the incubator garden over to the hard dirt pavilion where several tables form a border around the edge — everything from the public library to a lady taking your blood pressure, to *quinceañera* baubles, to vegetables, the orchard's seasonal fruit stand, and, at the far end near the parking lot, a food truck with coffee, bagels and burritos.

Otoña looks up from behind the vegetable table. I can't quite figure out her feelings — guarded? grateful? She's not letting on, not just yet. But she does seem surprised to see Marley.

CeCe grins from ear to ear. "Hello, Dad," she says ever so charmingly. Spotting Marley, she asks, "Who is this? Can I pet him?"

Zach pats Marley reassuringly. "Marley, I would like you to meet my daughter, Cecelia. CeCe, this is Marley, my PTSD Service Dog. And yes, you can pet him." CeCe fondles Marley's head and tickles him behind the ears. A little excessive, from my point of view. But if it keeps the peace, It's OK.

"Would you like to buy some vegetables, Dad? I have some wonderful selections here. The price is — well, you donate what you feel is right." She stops, that grin plastered all over her face that she obviously can't contain.

"Well, don't mind if I do, young lady," says Daddy Zach, as if he'd come straight from the Queen of England's school of manners. "What do you recommend? Or perhaps your mama can give me some ideas." He looks cautiously at Otoña.

"Hello, Zachariah," she says quietly. "I'm glad to see you. That sure is a handsome dog you have with you."

I practically drop my mythical socks. This is not what I expected. But Big Joe has a way with folks. Apparently Marley does too. I feel a bit jealous, but I get over it.

Marley, a handsome (for a dog) golden retriever, lays down at Zach's feet.

"Otoña, I am glad to see you as well," Zachariah answers.

There is a stillness at this table, like the angels stopped beating their wings.

Suddenly, from across the dirt floor, the noise of a shrill whistling whine explodes, triggered by an interruption between the mic and the monitors.

Marley lets out a shrill bark and jumps to his feet, searching for danger.

Zachariah whips around as if an incoming bomb has landed right behind him. Right away he realizes it was the malfunctioning mic over by Hurricane. He closes his eyes, clenches his hands. "Breathe deep, soldier," he whispers to himself. He inhales deeply, three times, and exhales slowly each time. He breathes in again and lets out a long low sigh. He opens his eyes, unclenches his hands, and turns back to the vegetable table. Marley stays by his side, then reassured that the danger has passed, utters a low "woof, woof," and lies back down.

From the corner of my eye, I notice Otoña watching intently as he turns, clenches, breathes, lets out that sigh, unclenches, and turns back to the table, his emotions contained. He pats Marley. "Thanks, buddy, it's OK. False alarm."

I must admit, that was pretty cool teamwork.

Chapter 30

Community Garden #104: A Good Recipe

The music gets back on course as Zorro and Hurricane blast out some Hip Hop. The juvenile almost-were or have-beens saunter over from the incubator farm and start making their moves around the speakers.

From a feline viewpoint, this is nuts. But, as it happens, who cares? All the humans around me burst out laughing, and in the place of stillness is a comfortable ease. *Purr.* I'm down with comfortable ease.

Zachariah turns to Big Joe and asks, "Didn't you say you had a great stir-fry recipe for the guys at the halfway house? Maybe Otoña has a bunch of those veggies." It's a coup for Zachariah — he has smoothed the silence into a friendly and useful conversation.

Otoña offers her two bits. "I know a good one that will use several of what we have here. You could take two onions, and a few carrots, and then the broccoli, and" — as CeCe puts the veggies in a bag, she hesitates — "would you like to add some sugar snap peas? They're not quite the thing to put with broccoli, but they're all so good, and they're just at the end of the season. No more until late fall."

Zachariah smiles. "Sure, why not? Sounds delicious. My buddies over there will be happy to have something other than deep-fried."

CeCe puts all the produce in a large paper bag that does *not* split open. She's packed well.

Daddy Zach asks, "How much?"

CeCe bats her eyelashes. "We just accept donations."

"Here." Zach lays a $20 on the counter and picks up the bag. "Thanks for helping me plan dinner tonight."

Otoña looks at the $20. "That's mighty generous. Thank you! Have a good dinner."

Another pause — again broken by the raucous Hip Hop from the other side of the arena. Zorro has finally figured his dad is at Mom and CeCe's table and he comes over to give him a macho fist-bump. Introductions between Zorro and Marley go smoothly. I can tell that Marley is really a pro at keeping it chill when there's no danger.

"Hey, you're getting taller," ventures the dad.

"Since last week?" Zorro pokes Daddy Zach in the ribs.

Big Joe has let things unfold on their own. Now he pipes up, "OK, guys, I gotta go. Zach, coming with me? Marley, you too?"

"Sure. Thanks for the veggies, 'Toña, good to see you. And kiddos — CeCe and Zorro — next time be ready to show me your artwork." They both grin, look at each other, and nod. Zorro whispers to his sister, "I *knew* it was him!"

I can't hear what Otoña says, because she says it very softly. But she looks straight at Zachariah, and her gaze lingers. She might be saying, "I hope I'll see you again, Zach." But someone near the veggie sink splashed mud on me and I curve around to lick myself clean, so I can't be sure.

CeCe sneaks around the table and hugs her dad. "Have a great dinner tonight," she says. "I love you, Dad. Bye, Marley."

Between the juvenile delinquents, ex-cons, vet with PTSD, do-good college kids, grey-haired bank lady, university and church volunteers, the struggling single mom with newly-dubbed teenagers, me, and (I must admit) Marley, the service dog, the garden is a place where everyone is part of the community — a true *community* garden.

Chapter 31

The Real Reward

So, we're back where we started — at the
awards ceremony. It's Memorial Day weekend,
and about a hundred humans have gathered
to clap a lot and listen to long speeches. As I
said, there's Madam Mayor, the Bank CEO, the
University President, and Captain Chris himself from the Veterans'
Volunteer group. Interns and volunteers from churches, high schools,
corporations, the local botanical garden, and government agencies
populate the entire pavilion.

What has been achieved? They've got a real community garden
going. They've figured out how to store trash from the kitchen in a
compost heap, add cardboard, chicken poop and water and turn it
into rich compostable mulch to add to the soil.

They've learned that water can be controlled through piping
and drip hoses to use less but grow more. They've found a way for
the big institutions to help in major ways — from the re-purposed
irrigation pipe to the installation of a refrigerator room and two large
sinks to wash produce. They've fixed the honeybee situation. A new
muscovy duck is living proof that the bees and the birds can co-exist.
Zorro has helped Wiley create a "People's Mural."

They've also added bathrooms for the humans. Yay!

Most of all, they've figured out how people can learn to be steady
and reliable while learning how to feed themselves and give back
to their community. Church volunteers and ex-felons finally back
on the 'outside' are working alongside each other, sharing time and
skills. 'Kids at risk' are cooling their heels. Folks who speak languages
from different countries find, in the garden, a common lingo. And
Big Joe has set Zachariah and Otoña on a path to reconciliation of

some kind, because they both love their children. If you check the body language, you know they love each other too.

Joe sticks out an arm and waves at Zach to come closer. With Marley at his side, Zach edges around the crowd and positions himself respectfully at one end of the veggie table, while Otoña oversees the other, arms linked between Darlene and Latifa.

Cece moves over to lean comfortably against her dad. Zorro had put a can of tuna from Dady Zach under the table for me and handed a big doggie bone to Marley. Marley and I eye each other — cautiously at first — and then focus on our own treats. Mine smells great — it's albacore! He seems more interested in chewing and slobbering. Meanwhile, as long as I'm not a threat to Zach (which is never!), Marley is not a threat to me. We're chill, and all is right with the world.

The University president makes introductions. He lavishes praise on all the adult key players. As far as I can tell, the 'key players' are the rich and famous, but not really the individuals who I have seen put in their time to grow the food — the do-gooders, 'developmentals,' and delinquents. There is a nod to Big Joe, but no mention of Zorro or CeCe, and not even a glance at me.

After a few more speeches, Ms. Mayor cedes the mic to Big Joe. He takes a broad look around the pavilion, nods to CeCe, Zorro, and Zach, and catches my eye. He praises just about everyone under the tarp. Finally, holding the plaque aloft, he says, "Now it is time to announce the one — or two, or three — with the most community spirit, those who have done the most this year to forge this former dump into a thriving community garden. It is my distinct honor to bestow the first Annual Community Garden Service Award upon"….

We'll leave it there. You know who really deserves it.

Author's Afterword

Perhaps the most obvious fictionalization in *FINDING ZACHARIAH* is that while our story occurs during a period of twelve months, the community gardens which inspired this story took closer to fifteen years in the making. The work continues.

You may think having the feral cat as narrator is fiction. But I've met him.

The brindle is both true *and* a metaphor.

The theme of people coming together and working successfully, getting along, even reconciling painful differences in order to make a community garden — and life — work successfully is both deeply true and also a sometimes-daunting challenge. After all, as Sebastian has observed, we are human.

As a feral cat, Sebastian was not much interested in the mighty powers that had an enormous influence on making this garden a success instead of another commercial venture. That threat always looms in the background. These large organizations are vitally important to any garden's success. Finally, a community garden of this size would be impossible to sustain without a lot of charitable donations of time, volunteers, supplies and financial support. A large thank you goes out in many directions.

As a culture and society, millions of us humans seem to be moving away from getting our hands in the dirt, leaving agriculture to big business and the low-paid immigrants who work harder, under tougher conditions, than most of us ever want to do.

However, by participating in our own back yard or a community garden, we can experience the satisfaction of growing our own tomatoes or broccoli, or whatever grows well in any particular ecological neighborhood 'zone'. We hope this little story will be a spark that ignites more efforts in more backyards and more communities — for both gardening and community.

Acknowledgements

This book is the result of help from many people, who brought different talents and contributions. I was not always able to get official names — sometimes just nicknames. Every person and organization mentioned has either worked in 'the garden' or contributed to this story in some way.

Thanks to: Abdul (aka Mr. Okra); Scott Abrahams, Founder, TeaCo Biological Supply; Adrian the 'Burma Tiger'; Keosha Anderson; John Wann Angeles; Anubis; Armrish; Michael Arnold; Bruce Babcock; Becca Berry, DGB volunteer; Brandon Bates; Bob; David Bock, Public Safety Liaison, Community Medical Services; Knoye Brown;; Reyna Butler, Public Lands Interpretive Association Outreach Coordinator; Diane Campoy; DBG volunteer; Paul Catalino (NRCS, USDA); Darren Chapman (CEO, Tiger Mountain Foundation); Deborah Kidd Chapman; Chingweh Cheng (@ asu.edu); Anne Cimarelli-Stears; Tammy Crosby; Carol Diemer; Stephanie Duarte (Tiger Mountain Foundation); Carlos Garcia; James Gentry; Harold Gossett; Peter Griffeth; Derrick Gutierrez, artist; Sarah Jamaica, U of A extension: Jemeesha; Jesenia; Katarina "K.J." Jones; Kiosha; Heather Okvat; Phebe Packer; Alexis Parker; Bridget Pettis and the Bridget Pettis Foundation; Katelyn Prinzo (Agribusiness Manager at Tiger Mountain Foundation); Sai Rajesh and the Sri Sathya Saibaba Global Community (SSSGC); Milena Riegel; Olivia Smith and Marshall; Rodney Eugene Smith; Rebecca de la Torre (USDA); Gerardo Vasquez; Robert Wilson (USDA); Roosevelt Wright; and Emily Yulga (USDA).

Several readers have made a significant difference in helping me improve the quality and accuracy of **ZACHARIAH** — Steve Cosumano; Carol Diemer; Phebe Packer; Marilee and Steve Orcutt; Tom Cameron; Francie Randolph; and Cindy Yurth. And to Becky Norwood at Spotlight Publishing House, who ultimately made this book possible. Thank you, thank you. Still, all errors are my own.

Several local and national organizations are critical to our understanding of gardens — all aspects of what goes into a garden. They include: Arizona Department of Agriculture; Arizona Game and Fish; Arizona State University School of Sustainability; The Audubon Society; City of Phoenix Water and Sewer Department; Desert Botanical Garden; Liberty Wildlife; Maricopa County; The Nature Conservancy; Northrup King's Arizona Planting Guide for Phoenix; Orchard Community Learning Center; Roosevelt School District; Students for Ethical Donations (SEED); Tiger Mountain Foundation; Unity: Unlimited Potential; United States Department of Agriculture; and University of Arizona Agricultural Extension Service.

They may not even know they are vitally important, but we have drawn on their many resources, with gratitude for the fine research and dedicated work that goes into all aspects of a successful community garden.

Glossary

Note: these definitions are gleaned from a few different published dictionaries, Wikipedia, and other general sources. While there is an effort to be scientifically accurate, complete accuracy and general descriptions may be incomplete. For the curious, continue to do research!

Abandoned: left or forsaken completely; possession surrendered absolutely.

Aka: also known as.

Animals: members of the **Domain Eukaryote,** the **Kingdom Animalia,** animals are multicellular, mostly consuming organic material (plants or animals), and breathe oxygen.

Berm: an edge or shoulder of ground running alongside a canal or ditch.

Biodegrade: decaying and being absorbed by the environment, such as paper and kitchen scraps, and as opposed to aluminum cans and many plastics.

Brindle: grey or tawny with lighter and darker streaks or spots.

Carnivore: any chiefly flesh (meat)-eating mammal of the order Carnivora, such as dogs, cats, bears, seals and weasels.

Caterwaul: a powerful wail by a cat, usually from fear or displeasure.

Chlorophyll: The green coloring matter of leaves and plants, essential to the production of carbohydrates by **photosynthesis** (see **photosynthesis**) and occurring in a bluish-black form.

Coagulate, Coagulating: to change from a fluid into a thickened mass, to curdle, congeal — like blood from a wound.

Community: A social, religious, occupational or other group sharing common characteristics or interests.

Companion Plants: Plants that, when grown together or near each other, have a beneficial effect, one on the other, as in on repelling garden pests (including insects, some worms, etc.) that are harmful to the other, or one attracting pollinators that are beneficial to the other.

Compost: A mixture of various decaying organic substances such as dead leaves, manure, or vegetable leftovers.

Crepuscular: Relating to or resembling twilight, dim, indistinct; also, for certain animals, appearing or active in the twilight.

Cultivate: To prepare or work on land to prepare it for planting and raising crops; promoting or improve the growth of plants, by labor and attention.

Decompose (with plants): to disintegrate, rot, putrefy, or resolve into parts or elements that did make the whole.

DMZ: De-militarized zone, used to describe an area between two groups or areas not at peace with each other, such as North and South Korea.

Domestic: Tame, domesticated, a "domestic" animal such as a cat, dog, cow or horse.

Eukaryote: A single- or multi-celled organism whose cells contain a distinct membrane-bound nucleus. All plants, animals and fungi are Eukaryotes.

Fauna: The animals of a given region.

Feral: Existing in a natural or wild state; having reverted to a wild state, as from domestication, as a "feral" cat.

Flora: The plants of a particular region.

Fraternal (as in twins): one of a pair of twins, not necessarily resembling each-other, that develop from two fertilized ova or eggs.

Fungus, fungi (plural): any of numerous **thallophytes** of the **Kingdom** Fungi, including mushrooms, molds, mildews, rusts, smuts, characterized chiefly by an absence of vascular tissue and of **chlorophyll**, and subsisting upon dead or living organic matter. (See **thallophyte, chlorophyll**).

Guano: A natural manure composed chiefly of the excrement ("poop") of seabirds and bats.

Habitat: The native environment of an animal or plant; the kind of place that is natural for the life and growth of an animal or plant.

Herbivore, Herbivorous: Pertaining primarily to hoofed animals who feed on plants. The horse is a herbivore, the horse is herbivorous.

Identical (as in twins): a pair of twins of the same sex or gender, usually resembling one another closely, that develop from a single fertilized ovum or egg.

IED: Improvised Explosive Device, often used by local opposition to the official troops, these devices could be home-made, thus available to local guerrillas and terrorists. They were often planted by roadsides and would blow up tanks and trucks that ran over them

Instinct: 1) An inborn pattern of activity or tendency to action common to a given biological species; 2) a natural or innate impulse, inclination or aptitude.

Manna: From the Bible, a delicious food miraculously supplied to the Israelites in the wilderness.

Mentor: Someone who acts as a wise and trusted guide or advisor.

Nocturnal: As to animals, active by night.

Nutrients: nourishing, providing nourishment, a nutrient substance.

Omega-3: a polyunsaturated fatty acid, essential for normal retinal function, that influences reduced blood-cholesterol levels, and inflammatory and immune reactions.

OMG: Oh my gosh, oh my god, an exclamation of surprise.

Omnivore: a person or animal that eats both animal and plant foods.

Organic: Existing in or derived from plants, animals and all other compounds of carbon.

Organism: form of life, such as any plant or animal, that ic composed of mutually dependent parts that maintain various vital processes.

Papillae on cat's tongue to lick meat from bones and to groom its coat.

Photosynthesis: The **synthesis** (combining) of complex organic materials, especially carbohydrates, from carbon dioxide, water and inorganic salts, using sunlight as the source of energy and with the aid of a **catalyst** (that which causes activity between two or more persons or forces without itself being affected)) such as chlorophyll.

Plants: Organisms of the **Eukaryote Domain,** members of the **Kingdom Plantae,** are predominantly photosynthetic, getting their energy from the sunlight, producing chlorophyll.

Pollinator: an organism that transfers pollen from the **anther** (the pollen-bearing part of the stamen of a plant) to the **stigma** (the part of a plant pistil which received the pollen) of a flower. Bees, moths and butterflies are major pollinators of flowers and vegetables.

Predator: In relation to animals, one organism (one animal) that captures and feeds on others (e.g., a hawk is a predator feeing on mice, small birds and other animals).

Prey: An animal hunted or seized for food, especially by a carnivorous animal. Rabbits and mice are generally prey of other predator animals.

Putrefy: To cause to rot or decay with an offensive odor.

Species: The major subdivision of a genus (classification), composed of related individuals that resemble one another and are able to breed among themselves but not able to breed with members of another species.

Taxonomy: The science of classification of organisms.

Thallophyte: Any plant of the phylum or division *Thallophyta,* comprising of algae, fungi and lichens.

Vitamins: Any of a group of organic substances that are essential in small quantities to normal health; Minerals are any of a class of substances occurring in nature, usually comprising inorganic substances.

Vole: a small mouse-like or rat-like rodent.

Zone: 1) any continuous area that differs in some way from other areas such as a demilitarized zone between two hostile countries; 2) any specific ecological zone with specific factors such as heat, annual rainfall, length of growing season, etc.

Questions for the Curious

- Why is it useful or important to distinguish between wild, domestic, abandoned and feral cats? What are the similarities? What are the differences?
- What plants grow best in cool weather (in your geographic zone)? Which grows best in warm weather?
- Are there plants that cannot grow well, or at all, in your geographic zone? What are the factors that influence their ability to grow in your area? (Consider amount of sun, temperature range, amount of water needed, drought tolerant, freeze tolerant, etc.)
- What are some companion plants to various vegetables? What do they do? Why are they called 'companion plants'? Learn more about companion plants for the vegetables in your garden.
- What is a 'pollinator plant'? Name three that grow well in your area.
- What kind of watering system do the vegetables in this community garden depend on — rain? flood irrigation? drip irrigation? other? (This may be a trick question, because there may not be just one answer for all plants).
- Not all birds are alike. Compare and contrast two birds mentioned in this garden.
- What ingredients make good compost? What proportion of compost should you mix into your existing soil?
- Name at least one state agency and one federal agency that may provide help and useful information to gardeners in your area. Are there any universities that also help gardeners and farmers?
- Why put kale in a smoothie?

Sources and Resources

Books, magazines, websites are all listed together alphabetically.

https://www.akc.org/expert-advice/training/service-dog-training-101/.

https://www.almanac.com/companion-planting-guide-vegetables.

AN IMMENSE WORLD, Ed Yong, New York, Random House, 2022.

ARBORETUM at Flagstaff, Pollinator Day information sources, June 2022.

BATS, rev. ed., M. Brock Fenton, Fitzhenry & Whiteside; Markham, Ontario, Canada, 2001.

BAT WATCHING AREA, posted signs by Arizona Game and Fish in the Flood Control District of Maricopa County, est. 1959, near 44th St. & Camelback Road, Phoenix.

"Beehives have Landed at Liberty Wildlife," by Amanda Harder, Guest Author, *WING BEATS*, Liberty Wildlife, Phoenix, AZ., @ 2022.

"Bumble Bees are Essential: Helping Pollinators Thrive," Saint Louis Zoo and the North American Pollinator Protection Campaign (undated, c. 2023).

CALL of the CATS: What I Learned about LIFE and LOVE from a FERAL COLONY, Andrew Bloomfield, New World Library, Novato, CA, 2016.

CAT DADDY, by Jackson Galaxy with Joel Derfner, Jeremy P. Tarcher; Penguin, New York, 2012.

COMMUNITY CATS: A Journey into the World of Feral Cats, by
Anne E. Beall, Ph.D., iUniverse Star, NY, 2014.

DESERT BOTANICAL GARDEN, 1201 N Galvin Pkwy, Phoenix,
AZ.

Dictionary.com. (app).

Encyclopedia, The World Book, ©1992 (Chicago, London, Sydney,
Toronto); Bird, Insect, Spiders, Scorpion, Tarantula.

"Environmentally Friendly Landscaping," by Jasmine Bible,
NEST Magazine, courtesy of Jono Friedland, Spring/Summer 2022.

EPA: The United States Environmental Protection Agency
"Composting," "What is Composting?" "Why Compost at Home?"
"Options," "Your Backyard," "What you Can Compost -and What
to Avoid Composting at Home," "Steps for Backyard Composting,"
"Avoiding Rodents," "Worm Composting (Vermi-composting),"
"Benefits of Using Your Finished Compost."

https://www.epa.gov/recycle/composting-home.

GARDEN OF TOMORROW, 18th Street & Broadway, Phoenix,
AZ.

The *GREAT BACKYARD BIRD COUNT,* organized by the
Cornell University Lab of Ornithology, in Ithaca, NY, along with
the National Audubon Society and Birds Canada, from **"At year
25, Backyard Bird Count shows power of 'citizen science',"** Julia
Rubin, AP, *Arizona Republic* Weekend 02/18/23.

"Get A Green(er) Thumb," *Reader's Digest,* May 2024.

How Animals Understand the World, by Ed Wong, *Atlantic
Monthly,* July/August 2022.

How Cats See the World *www.Livescience.com* on feline vision.

How Community Gardens Work, by Louise Spilsbury, Gareth Stevens Publishing, New York, NY, 2014.

"In Praise of Gnats," by Michael J. Plagens, *The Cactus Wren-Dition,* Maricopa Audubon Society, Spring, 2022.

Information on cats: *www.britannica.com.*

"Introduction to URBAN AGRICULTURE," by Damien Thompson, co-Founder of Frontline Farming, *NEST Magazine,* courtesy of Jono Friedland, Spring/Summer 2022.

"Inviting Bees to Your Property — NO FEAR OF STINGS!" Prepared by the Garden Task Force of the North American Pollinator Protection Campaign (NAPPC), c. 2023

Maricopa County Animal Care and Control Information on Community Cats.

Moringa oleifera, Wikipedia information on the moringa tree, 11/23/22.

National Geographic. Almost everything by NatGeo is useful - books, online, movies.

Northrup King flyer, *ARIZONA PLANTING GUIDE,* Phoenix, AZ (no date).

ORCHARD COMMUNITY LEARNING CENTER, 911 W. Baseline Road, Phoenix, AZ 85041; oclc911@gmail.com.

Owls in the Phoenix Mountains Preserve, Phoenix Mountains Preservation Council (PMPC) Newsletter, November/December 2022, p.4.

"Partner with APS to Protect Arizona's Pollinators," APS (c. 2023). "Plight of the Pollinator," Prepared by the Rights of Way Task Force of the North American Pollinator /campaign (NAPPC), c. 2023.

ROOSEVELT ELEMENTARY SCHOOL DISTRICT, Phoenix, AZ.

SALT RIVER PROJECT irrigation and electricity corporation, Maricopa County.

"**Service dogs** can reduce the severity of **PTSD for veterans,** according to **new research,**" *Arizona Daily Sun,* B5, Thursday, July 18, 2024.

SPACES OF OPPORTUNITY, 1200 West Vineyard, Phoenix, AZ 85041.

SSLUG (Students for Sustainable Living And urban Gardening), Northern Arizona University, Flagstaff.

"The Circle of Life," by Michael Ferguson, East Millerbrook Middle School, April 8, 2018, *YouTube.*

"The Climate Crisis is a Butterfly Crisis," Environmental Defense Fund, Washington, DC, c. 2023.

"THE RAPTORS OF KYLER NOE," Cactus Wren-Dition, Maricopa County Audubon Society, Summer, 2023.

The Random House COLLEGE DICTIONARY, Revised Edition, Jess Stein, Editor in Chief, New York, 1975.

TIGER MOUNTAIN FOUNDATION.

www.Trupanium.com. Website on pet health and care.

UNLIMITED POTENTIAL, serving the Latino population in South Phoenix.

Vegetable Gardening for Dummies, 3rd Ed. by National Gardening Association, Charlie Nardozzi, Wiley & Sons, New Jersey, 2021.

www.Worldwildlife.org. Website on tigers

TAXONOMY CHARTS

The full taxonomy on any plant, animal, fungus or other will include the following categories: Domain, Kingdom, Phylum, Class, Order, Family, Genus and species. The most commonly used descriptions, after the kingdoms of "plant" or "animal" (or "fungus"), are Genus and species.

Very basic definitions of **Plant, Animal, Fungus,** and **Eukaryote** can be found in the **Glossary.**

SAMPLE TAXONOMY CHART OF ANIMALS

	Italian Honey Bee	Feral Cat	Human Being	Mexican Free-Tailed Bat	Great Horned Owl
Kingdom	Animalia	Animalia	Animalia	Animalia	Animalia
Pyhlum	Anthropoda	Chordata	Chordata	Chordata	Chordata
Class	Insecta	Mammalia	Mammalia	Mammalia	Aves
Order	Hymenoptera	Carnivora	Primate	Chiroptera	Strigiformes
Family	Apidae	Felidae	Hominidae	Molossida	Strigidae
Genus	Apis	Felix	Homo	Tadaria	Bubo
Species	Mellifera lingustia	Catus (domesticus)	Sapiens	Brasiliensis	Virginianus

SAMPLE TAXONOMY CHART OF PLANTS

	Prickly Pear Cactus	Honey Mesquite Tree	Lemon Tree	Tomato	Zucchini
Kingdom	Plantae	Plantae	Plantae	Plantae	Plantae
Phylum	Magnollo-phyta	Tracheo-phyta	Tracheo-phyta	Spermato-phyta	Tracheo-phyta
Class	Magnolip-sida	Magnolip-sida Dicotyledoris	Magnolip-sida	Magnolip-sida Dicotyledoris	Magnolip-sida
Order	Caryo-pyhllales	Fables	Sapindales	Solanales	Cucur-bitales
Family	Cactaceae	Fabaceae	Rutaceae	Solanaceae	Cucur-bitaceae
Genus	Opuntia	Prosopis	Citrus	Solanun	Cucurbita
Species	Engel-manii	Glandulosa	Limon	Lycoper-sicum	Pepo

About the Author

Nancy Hicks Marshall grew up on Long Island, New York. Her father always planted an organic vegetable garden, from the "Victory Gardens" of World War II until his very later years. Moving to Phoenix in 1975, Nancy started a vegetable garden, finding the seasons and conditions dramatically different than that of the Northeast.

First, it is possible in Phoenix to plant in the fall (early October is good) and again in the winter (January, February), but it is difficult to grow much during the summer months. Second, in the dry climate there is not much natural decomposition, so it's important to add compost and other mulch to enrich and replenish the soil.

Nancy has had the opportunity to volunteer in two community gardens in South Phoenix. The science of planting, weeding mulching, and irrigating is an ongoing challenge for all the gardeners and farmers. In addition, when numerous individual persons and organizations come together to try and make such a garden work on an ongoing basis, we humans face all kinds of challenges. Two main benefits of working in a community garden are that we both produce healthy food for families, and we develop vital skills and productivity.

We hope **FINDING ZACHARIAH** has allowed you to capture some of the spirit of what is possible in a community garden.

About the Artist

Marie Provine has always made art, and more so since she ended her academic career at Arizona State University. She works in oil, pastel, watercolor on various themes often related to nature. Her work appears in local galleries, and she takes commissions.

Describing herself as an impressionistic realist, Provine strives to render personality and attitude in her animal subjects and to keep light and life in all her work.

She is president of the Tempe Artists Guild. In 2021, one of my watercolors was selected by the Arizona Citizens for the Arts to be awarded to a recipient at the Arizona Governor's Arts Awards March gala. Her art was featured in the Spring 2019 edition of *Emeritus Voices: The Art of Doris Marie Provine* and she enjoys juried membership status within the Arizona Art Alliance. This summer she was juried into the Arizona Art Alliance's summer exhibit: The Heat is On.

Other books by Nancy Hicks Marshall

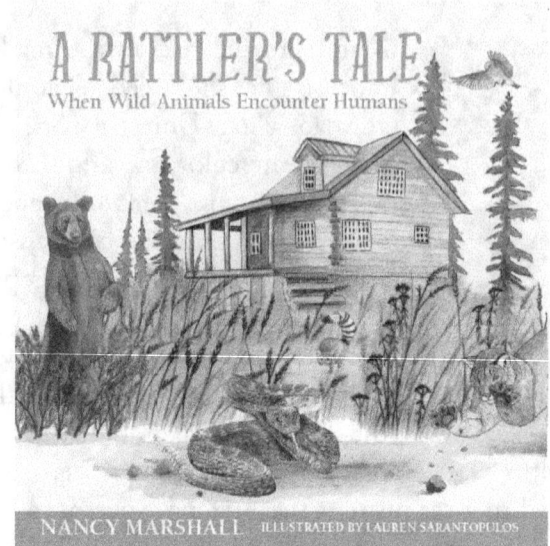

https://a.co/d/9UdhP9G

https://a.co/d/5JOVVps

THE BOOK OF PRO-s:

An Alphabetical Chat About Things We Can Like

Nancy Hicks Marshall

https://a.co/d/9UdhP9G

https://a.co/d/31stVDY

www.ingramcontent.com/pod-product-compliance
Lightning Source LLC
Chambersburg PA
CBHW071400170626
46811CB00003B/1193

* 9 7 8 0 9 8 2 8 2 5 9 7 6 *